BRAD

PERRY'S NEST BOOK 5

KATHI S. BARTON

This is a work of fiction. Names, characters, places, and incidents are products of the author's imagination or are used fictitiously and are not to be construed as real. Any resemblance to actual events, locations, organizations, or persons, living or dead, is entirely coincidental.

World Castle Publishing, LLC
Pensacola, Florida
Copyright © 2024 Kathi S. Barton
Paperback ISBN: 9798891262225
eBook ISBN: 9798891262232
First Edition World Castle Publishing, LLC, June 1, 2024
http://www.worldcastlepublishing.com
Licensing Notes
Cover: Karen Fuller
Editor: Karen Fuller

Prologue

"I'm here to deliver an order from the dairy warehouse. It's from Miller Farms." Dill handed over the paperwork to the man at the guardhouse. When he asked for her name and identification, she handed it over as well. Since she'd been doing this particular delivery for about five years now, she had all her things ready to hand over when asked. "I'm supposed to be here by noon, and it's just shy of that."

"They told me that you were coming in early for this one. I'm to tell you thanks and to give this to you." She was handed an envelope along with a gift card from the restaurant. "Mr. Kirk, he's in the warehouse right now and said to make sure that you get some food for you for coming in four hours early. We all appreciate it."

Dill put the card and the envelope over her visor and went to the dock door, she was told. Not a bad deal for getting on the road a few hours early, she thought. After backing into the space, she was getting ready to get out when her cell phone rang. She wouldn't do two things at once. It was difficult enough to get a trailer backed into a small space and then get the wheels locked and everything without being distracted. Answering the phone with her last name, she sat in the cab.

"Ms. Dillard." She said that it was her and that she wasn't going to be taking a long call to get to the point. "I like that. Right to the point. It's Brad Kirk. I wanted to personally thank you for today. You've saved our butts here."

"Like I told the guy out front, I had time, and I didn't mind. But Mr. Kirk, I can't get this ready for unloading while jawing around on the phone with you." She looked in the cab and saw that her son was awake now. "Is there anything else?" His laughter made her pissy, and she didn't know why.

"No. Nothing else. Go on. Get your work done. I'll talk to you later." She closed the connection and turned to Toby. He was getting his shorts on just as she was opening the door. Dill wondered what he thought they'd have to talk about but let it go. People said all kinds of weird things.

"Don't get out until I tell you." He said 'yes, mom' like he'd heard her say the same thing a hundred times. He probably had. Toby and she had been riding the roads since he was four weeks old, and she was fresh out of trucking school. "Don't eat much. They gave me a gift card for the place. I know you've been wanting to try it."

It took her nearly an hour to get her trailer locked and ready for unloading. The man on duty at the doors told her that it wouldn't be long, but he'd have her trailer pulled into the lot if she wanted to get some food. Glad for that, she told him where she was going to be. After getting her gear and her son, they were headed to the parking lot to see if there was room for the big rig.

They had been seated when she remembered the envelope. Stuffing it deeper into her backpack, she was talking to Toby about the menu when they both decided on the big brunch that was going on today. If they could stuff themselves enough, she knew that they'd not have to stop again until dinner. That was fine by her. She hated snacking on the road.

They were in line when she heard from the warehouse. Her load was emptied, and her trailer was in the lot. Glad for the knowledge that she'd be able to get out sooner than planned all the way around, Dill watched Toby fill his plate with two slices of pizza, three burgers, a large load of fries, as well as mashed potatoes, gravy, and fried chicken.

"You do know that we'll eat again, right?" Dill got a salad, something that she sorely missed while being on the road all the time. Toby got himself two glasses of milk and headed to their table. She'd bet her next check he'd be ready for another round of food by the time she got there.

Since it was so early in the day, the place was practically empty. When seated, they put her and Toby in one of the larger rooms alone, and she was glad for that. No one would be so close that she'd feel closed in. It was a problem that she had with larger restaurants. Especially ones with buffets. The room they'd been seated in was devoid of anyone but her and Toby.

"Ms. Kirk?" Dill glanced at the man standing

not a foot from her while she was putting croutons on her salad. "You've been difficult to find."

"My name is Becka Dillard. I don't know who you're looking for, but it's not me." He just laughed at her. Finishing up her salad, she turned and left the man there. She was just reaching out to her son when another man stepped in front of her. *"Toby, I want you to find a waitress and tell them that I'm in trouble here. That someone is looking for a woman by the name of Kirk and thinks it's me."*

She could see her son now, and when he nodded, wiped his mouth off, and stood up, she could have kissed him. As he made his way away from the table, she sat her plate down across from her son's and sat down, much to the anger of the two men.

"Ms. Kirk, you're not making this easy on yourself. We only want to talk." She told them that she had an ID and that she'd show it to them if they would just leave her alone. "I have ID too. It don't tell you shit about who I am. We just want to talk to you and then to your husband."

"I'm not married either." She slowly pulled her backpack to her front and slowly eased the zipper down. "I'm a self-employed driver. I don't have a spouse, nor do I have a company that I work for. You're making a mistake, and I'm only going to tell you one more time that I'm not who you're looking for."

"Bradley boy is going to make sure that we're paid this time." She told the second man that she was happy for him. Then, a gun appeared on the table, and she could feel one ramming into her ribs from behind. "You pull out anything other than a little bitty purse, and I'm going to blow your head off."

She shot the second man before he could wipe the fucking grin off his face. Her gun was pointed at the first guy's head. Really, she was pressing it into his forehead when someone cleared their throat from behind her. She didn't move but told whoever it was the same thing that she'd told the two men.

"I was in line when they approached me. The second one there, he threatened me. I don't take well to that. This guy, he said something about Bradley boy paying him. I just want to enjoy my first good meal in a long time with my son." She could smell Toby. "Are you all right, son?"

"Yes, ma'am. This man is going to help us.

He was at the cash register when I got there. He said that you know him." She didn't so much as take her eyes off the man in front of her. "See, I told you that she'd not care. Mom will kill this other man, too, if he don't put that gun down. She's not one to mess with."

"Toby." He said he was sorry, moved across from her, and resumed eating. "Really? You're going to enjoy your food now?"

"I might not be able to if you splatter that man's head all over me. This is the best fried chicken since your grannies. And you know how much I like that." He was calming her. Something that he did very well. *"Mom? Do you know Mr. Kirk?"*

"No." She heard the scrape of a chair and glanced at the man who sat next to her son. "You touch him, and I'll tear you apart."

"No one will bother him. On this, you have my word." Dill snorted at the man. "Someone else I know does that when she's disbelieving of something. You'd like her, I think."

"Doubtful. I don't suppose you've called the police, have you?" He said that he had, and when Toby offered him a piece of his chicken, she glared at the two of them. "This isn't a social event, young man. Eat so that we can get out of here when the police arrive."

"Since my mom is really busy right now, my name is Toby Dillard. I'm sixteen, and she's my mom, Becka Dillard. Not Rebecca, but just plain Becka." Mr. Kirk told him who he was. "Good to know. You might not care right at the moment but she's not really my mom but my aunt. My mom died when someone from another group decided that they'd do a better job than my dad and mom did and killed them off. If not for visiting my aunt, I might well have—"

"Toby, what are you doing?" He told her. She looked at the man for the first time. "Oh. I don't know anything about…please keep the information to a minimum if you don't mind. I don't care if he smells like home to you."

"Yes, ma'am." She watched her handsome nephew stand up and smile at her. "Since you have things under control, and I don't know when we might get to have a meal like this again, I'm going to go and get some more food. Just…if you'd not mind, Mom, please don't make more of a mess with this other guy's brains until I get done eating.

All right."

"I want you to know, young man, that I'm going to beat you senseless when we get out of this mess." As he walked by her, he kissed her on the top of her head, and she felt her eyes fill with tears. "That isn't buying you any points."

"Yes, ma'am, I know that. I'll be back." She glanced again at the man sitting there by where Toby had been.

"The police have pulled up and are now in the front of the restaurant. I want to thank you for not making it known throughout the place what's going on back here. This man," she watched the man she was holding the gun on head wobble when Mr. Kirk hit him, "He's going to jail for a long time. He is the reason, along with his buddy there on the floor, why we needed you to bring in our delivery earlier."

"I don't know them. But that man threatened me." He said that he knew that too. The police came, and she felt the bite of a gun put to the back of her head. "I have a license to carry, and that man—"

"Officer Hill, I want you to remove the gun from her head. I told the dispatcher when I called them that I had this under control. Remove your gun, or I will. And you know me well enough to understand that I'm not a man that likes to repeat myself." The gun pressure disappeared. Before she could ask what the hell was going on, Mr. Kirk began speaking again. "These are the two men that were on camera yesterday breaking into the back of the dairy area and pissing into the vats. My staff here worked through the night to get them serialized and ready for today's milk. I also told you that they'd be back and that they'd all but told us that they would. And today, not only did they show up, but they brought a gun into a very public place and threatened my patrons. Going so far as to make it so that one of my very loyal patrons had to kill one of them because you couldn't get up off your fat ass and make sure that the other people here were safe too." When Kirk stood up, she didn't move. Something was going on. A pissing contest, she thought, and it pissed her off that she was in the middle of it. Just as she was going to turn over whatever the hell was going on to the other officers standing around, a woman, a very beautiful and elegant woman, sat down when her son did.

"Mom, don't kill her." She glared at Toby and then asked him what he was doing. "I thought that since we more than likely won't be allowed to come back here anymore that I'd throw us a big party. This lady here, her name is Lander, I think she said, found me in line. I wouldn't have talked to her, but she's with this monster of a man, too, and I'm sort of afraid of him. He's filling up his plate along with hers."

"Toby, do you know that we're going to have to be here for a bit? I killed a man." He ate a chicken leg while he answered her. "I guess I need to practice more on knowing who is who then. No, I didn't know she was a vampire." She looked around at the open window shades. "How sure are you about that?"

"He's very sure. Why are you eating a salad when there is all this other food up there? I saw they had pudding. I love that stuff." She told the woman, not having any idea why she was what she'd been thinking about a salad. "How long have you two been on the road? I'm assuming it's been a while, right?"

"I was an infant when I was with her. She'd only just graduated from trucking college, and my mom and dad wanted to go out to a fancy dinner." Toby told the table the rest of the story, how he'd been with her and not dead when their bruin had been ambushed. When he pushed away his food, he looked at her. "If not for her all these years, sixteen on the road, I don't think that I'd be half the person that I am. I've called her mom from the start, and I don't know if I'd ever do anything different. She saved me."

No one said anything, and when the large man sat with them, he was talking to men and women in flak jackets with FBI and other initials on them when another woman sat down at the table. Toby, smiling, volunteered to go up and get another few plates of food when asked and came back with her a cup of hot tea. She really needed it about now.

Taking a lot less time than she thought that it might have, she was free to leave the bloodied table and enjoy some dessert. Not that she wanted any. She'd only been able to eat the salad because she'd been bullied into it. When Toby sat down next to her at the cleaned table, she hugged him to her.

"Did you want to hang out with Mr. Kirk?"

He said that he was planning a play date, no. "I don't know how that works. For all I know, you guys go around sniffing each other's asses all the time, and that's how you know each other."

"I promise you, there is no butt-sniffing. And Mr. Kirk isn't a real bear. He's friends with someone powerful, and they gifted him immortality. There's more to it than that, I'm sure, but for now, I'm ready when you are to get on the road." She didn't move but stared at him. "What?"

"Something happened? Did one of them... that woman, Lander, did she push you into something or say something to you? Where is she?" He pushed her back in the chair when she started after the woman. "Toby, you're all I have. I have to protect you."

"I don't know if you've noticed it or not, but I'm about a foot taller than you are and outweigh you by a good fifty or so pounds. And I can shift into a big black bear." She felt her eyes fill again. "Don't do that. If you do, then the two of us will be blubbering all over each other, and we'll not be able to find us a place to sleep tonight."

"I can cry. They said that we can sleep on the lot tonight." He held her to his chest, and she sobbed. It terrified her every time something out of the ordinary happened, and he might get hurt. "Your parents would have been so proud of you, honey. You know that, don't you?"

"I do. Even though I never had any memories with them, you've brought them alive for me every time we talk about them. Even if you're just— that's it, isn't it? I completely forgot. Today would have been her birthday." She nodded and tried very hard to keep herself under control for a few seconds. "Ah, Mom. You're the best. I don't think in all the world that anyone could have ended up with a better role model than what I've had all these years."

They ended up leaving the lot and finding them a nice little camping area. They no longer shared a tent, but she knew that he was close by. Just as she was coming back from the shower, a very much needed one, she saw that there was a large jeep in their spot. She didn't have to reach out to Toby to figure out what was going on. He was standing by the car, talking to a man next to him. It turned out to be Mr. Kirk.

~*~

He enjoyed talking to the young man. Toby was

personable as well as polite. Kirk thought that he was smart, too, but he, for some reason, kept it under his hat about that. When Dill, his aunt, joined them after changing into something less *jammie*, she called it, he thought that he could have stayed there forever.

"Why are you here?" He nearly laughed at her but didn't. She seemed to be on edge about something. It could have been the shooting, but he wasn't positive that was all of it. "You got all your delivery. The cops were taken care of. Though I will admit that it was nice seeing someone of authority get their comeuppance. So, again, why are you here? Toby and I aren't the kind of people men like you socialize with."

"I don't even want to hazard a guess at what you might mean by that. However, you're right. It is nice seeing the bad guys get what they deserve. But I'm here because I've been enjoying myself. Both this afternoon and now." Toby told his aunt to chill. "No, don't tell her that. She's just protecting herself and you. And from what I've seen, she's done a good job of both. No, I'm a wealthy man who doesn't get to hang out with someone around a campfire. Ever, I don't think. But even with all the crap going on today, I've really enjoyed your company. By the way, did you open the envelope? I was asked by my secretary to remind you about it?"

"It was something from my attorney." She'd opened it in the bathroom in case it was bad news. "It's all fine."

Brad didn't think it was anything near all fine, but he nodded. "I swear to you, Becka, I have no other motives here but to have a nice relaxing evening with a couple of nice people." She stood up, and he did as well. "Did I say something wrong?"

"No. I'm tired. I have a long drive tomorrow, and I have to get up early enough to go and get my trailer from the lot." She hugged Toby, then told him thanks for the food, and she was gone. She told Toby not to stay up too late. He had homework.

"You online school?" Toby said that he was a freshman in college and was taking a few classes through the summer. "Good job on that."

The two of them sat there for another two hours, just talking. He really didn't want to go home. And thought very seriously about driving a few spaces away and sleeping in his car so that he could —

"Mr. Kirk, my aunt made sure when I was younger to have spent time with a burin. She did it because I'm a bear, and I had questions that she didn't know. My dad changed my mom when they met so the two of them could run the burin together. I got a lot of questions answered while there, and I'd like to think I'm a bit more knowledgeable than most. All right?" Brad said that she'd been smart for doing that. Even though he'd been gifted a lot of magic and other things from a powerful burin, he knew very little about them. "Yeah, I kind of got that. You don't know crap, if you don't mind me saying so."

Brad laughed a little, and the two of them sat there for a little while longer before he realized that he was staring at Becka's tent again. He'd been thinking all kinds of odd thoughts about her since she'd gone to bed. When Toby said his name, he looked at the young man.

"I don't want to upset you none here, but you're my aunt's mate. You know that, don't you?" Brad laughed, thinking that this was a good joke that the kid had. "I'm not kidding you, Mr. Kirk. I could smell it on the two of you. She won't figure it out either unless I tell her, but I think that you need to be told. Before someone else tells you. I have a feeling that the people with you today would make fun of you for not figuring it out on your own."

"Yes. Relentlessly." He looked at Becka's tent and then at Toby again. "How sure are you about this? As you've already said, I don't know crap."

"You're her mate. She's not going to be happy and come to you with open arms like some other woman might. She's been hurt. Still is if I don't miss my bet. This man, I don't know his name other than Danny, has been—it's why we travel and do not have a space of our own. He's been...I've never told her this, and I won't unless I have to, but when her home burnt to the ground, I could smell him and the others then. Then, about five years ago, I noticed his scent around the truck and cab, too. He's trying to get in." He felt his need to protect the two of them roar up. "Calm it down, or she'll come out here. She's got a bit of magic; she can talk to me when necessary, but she can also feel me when I get stressed. And you're stressing me a little."

"I'm assuming that's part of the mate stuff." Toby smiled at him and nodded. "I didn't know. I mean, I've been thinking about her a lot, but I thought I was just enjoying her company. Which I am. Both of you. But this mating information? It's nothing that I thought of."

"I think I figured that out, too." They both laughed, and he felt better for it. "Those people you were with today, one of them smelled of bear. I know that none of them were bears, but they've had close contact with one. Do you know that person, too?"

"I do. I've only just met him. Well, the two of them. One is his mate, the other is a friend of ours. It's Calhoun Meyer. Have you heard of him?" Toby stared at him with an open mouth. "I'm going to take that as a yes. He's the king of the bruins."

"I know that. Every bear knows that, too." Toby leaned back in his chair and looked about as shell-shocked as he was feeling about finding out that he had a mate. "I don't want to tell you what to do here, but that man is wanting something from my aunt. If you can protect her, then I'm going to…do you really know King Meyer?"

"I do. Would you like to meet him?" Toby

nodded, then shook his head so many times Brad didn't know what he wanted. "He can do that pop-in thing. If I call him here, he'll...I don't know what he'll do, actually. As I said, I've only just met him."

They talked for a bit longer. When Toby said he was going to hit the bed, Kirk asked if he could sit there for a bit longer. Telling him to just be careful had him shaking hands with the young man. He really was a good kid. It wasn't until he exhausted every question and gotten no answers he had about mates that he knew he reached out to the only other person that he'd come to think of as his best friend. Hamish would have answers. If he didn't, then he'd know where to get them.

Getting into his car, he did what he'd been thinking. Drove to a few empty spaces down and pulled into the lot. While sitting there, he tried to reason with himself and tell himself that she was going to be all right until morning. But it didn't work. Brad was worried about his new little family now and that it would be the same in the morning.

After reaching out to his friend, he told him everything. Not just the fact that he had to be told she was his mate but about the man trying to get into her rig. Then, when he thought that he'd exhausted himself, he told him again how much he'd enjoyed talking to the two of them and hadn't any idea that he'd just found her and that she had him a son.

"I'd not start out with that if I were you." He asked which part when Hamish just showed up in the front seat of his car. "None of it. I mean, you'll tell her sometime, but I'd hold off about how her nephew had to tell you about her. Women can be touchy about the strangest things. Don't tell her that either. That will get us both in hot water."

"There seems to be a lot of things about women that scare you, too. Are you sure that you're the big badassed vamp, or is it, Lander?" He didn't even hesitate and said it was all Lander. "You're off your head if you ask me. And not all that helpful. The sixteen-year-old kid was more helpful than you are being."

"Then go wake him up so that you piss off his aunt." They both sat there for several seconds before they laughed. "Lander did some research on the two of them. When I left her, she was still digging. She told me about the murder and killing at the bruin. The burin has since been taken apart.

She didn't know why and said she'd get with Calhoun in the morning. That's all I can tell you about that. Becka is pretty much an open book, she said. There is nothing in her closet, it seems. I know that when I tell her about Becka being your mate, she'll dig deeper. Not that I think she'll find anything else."

"This is the strangest thing that has ever happened to me." They both sat there, staring into the darkness. "She's very beautiful. Smart and has done a better than average job on…how do I tell if what Toby told me is right? I mean, what if he's mistaken?"

"Do you feel like he might be?" Brad shook his head. "Then I'd take what he said as gospel. Hang on. I'm talking to Lander."

While his friend spoke to his mate, Brad got out of the car. He should have put her up in a hotel when he realized how chilly it was outside. But the two of them, she and Toby, seemed to be thrilled with camping out. Toby told him that it was nice to be able to have nature right there with them. He loved that part, too, but in small doses. He wasn't sure how he felt about camping out in the woods. He liked his comforts and didn't think he'd like doing this night after night.

Smiling, he told himself that he'd get used to it if that was what it took to make her happy. Brad laughed. Christ, he was getting to be as sappy as his friends with mates. He couldn't wait to figure out the other things that he'd heard about over the centuries. Also, he would have to figure out a way to tell her how old he was, too. That, he thought, was one of the many things that he'd put off as he'd been advised. But he would ask his son too when he—

"Lander wants to talk to you." He nodded and got back into the car. Whatever advice she had for him, he'd use it. She was a good deal smarter than her mate, as he knew Becka would be to him.

Chapter 1

Brad felt terrible for what was going on with Becka, his mate and the new to the family. There were a total of thirteen files in front of her, plus the one in her hand. Each one of them, all labeled with a sticky note, told her not only things that she needed to know but things that she would need to take care of in the immediate future. There was also the issue that some of it had come to her too late for her to have been able to do anything with it. The filing of the birth certificate of her nephew, as well as her adoption of him, had been taken care of by my Launder. All the paperwork had been filed away so that no one was the wiser about it not being done before. Brad was happy about that. One small detail that neither one had to worry over.

With everything going on when Toby was born it had been difficult for her—nay, impossible for her to have done anything about that part of her raising the young man. Both his parents and grandmother had been brutally murdered while she'd been babysitting him. Not only the three of them but the entire pack had been murdered, including the children, in the most heinous way imaginable. If he could, he'd hunt all the men down who had been responsible and murder them in the same ways.

Brad was having a hard time gauging her reactions right now. They'd only known one another a few weeks, and most of that had been with her being an over-the-road trucker who had been working for him without his knowledge for the last few years. Laughing, he thought that he'd not want to play any games of chance with her until he got to know her better. Maybe not even then.

When she picked up one of the files that had been marked with an address, she asked Launder how they were able to figure this out. Brad could see from where he was sitting that it was an address that seemed familiar to him. Then, he only just remembered what the address meant when Becka spoke. That not only had arson been the cause of the fire that took her home and only stationary place for her, but they also had a good idea of how it had started. She'd lost everything in the fire. And Brad would bet that she'd say that it was worth it to have been able to save Toby from the same death as his parents had had to endure.

"I didn't know about it until I started digging into your past. I must say, I'm pretty impressed with your driving record as an over-the-road driver. I didn't know if you were the norm or not in never having a ticket, but it was pointed out to me that you'd not have had any serious accidents either. Congratulations on that, Becka. You should be proud of yourself. I would imagine that has a great deal to do with Toby riding with you all the time." Becka glanced at Toby and then nodded. "As for knowing who might have set the fire, that came from Toby. He told Brad that he smelled the man that was around your truck recently as well. That's when we were able to attach his name to a few other things that had gone on around the area." This time, she really looked hard at her nephew.

"Yeah, it's nice that he's so forthcoming with his information, isn't it?" It didn't take a rocket scientist to hear the sarcasm dripping off of each word. He had a feeling that Toby was going to be in the dog house for a good long time because he did not share information with his aunt that could have been lifesaving. Lucky for all of them, neither of them had been hurt and that was because the two of them kept an eye on each other while out on the road. "What do we know about this Danny person other than he's not a bear, but he has several bear friends? I'm assuming more than I have."

"You're being very calm." Becka glared at him, and Brad laughed. "I'm sorry. But I'm barely holding onto my anger about what they did to you, and you're very calm looking. You've had less time to deal with this mentally than I have, and I'm still raging inside how they screwed the two of you over."

"I'm far from calm. However, what you just said isn't true. I've had a little bit longer to deal with this than you have simply because I've had to be on my guard all the time. I might not have known the players that were around, but I did know that we were being watched all the time. They took everything from Toby and me when they burnt down my home in addition to his family home as well." She looked at Launder, Hamish's mate, and asked her if she was sure she needed the details about the sloth that had been destroyed the night that Toby's parents had been bears with, too. "The only reason that I have any idea what went down is because when I sent Toby to the then-local sloth of a friend of mine, he took me aside and told me everything he knew. Which is a great deal more than the police did. He was also able to get me some information about Toby that I didn't have. Weight and things like that. It had been filed with the local doctor's office, and he found me a copy so that I could get him registered for the doctor's office. Then later to get him into school."

"Were they all killed to take over the sloth? That is one thing that I'd like to know." So did he, but Hamish would get more answers from the king of the bears rather than just him. He wasn't even sure that Becka was going to answer him when she got up to pace, something that he noticed that Toby did as well. "I'm assuming that you've had your ear to the ground for some time now. At least sixteen years, correct?"

"More than I think most have, yes. Liza and Roman Jermon had been married for two years when they found out they were going to have a baby—Toby. Liza is...was my sister, and I couldn't have been happier for them than I was at their wedding. Then, just a few years later, they had Toby." Calhoun, the king of the bears, asked if Toby knew anything about that day or the days before and after. "He does. Of course, he didn't then. He'd only been an infant. And I don't know how well I would have been at keeping him safe if not for staying with Liza when he was born. Changing diapers and that sort of stuff is not intuitive, no matter what people think. Besides, I would never keep something like that from him. The issues came up at one of the schools he attended and I had a duty to his parents to tell him what had happened. The real truth of it. I think that it helped him a great deal, or perhaps not that he didn't remember them at all. He was sorry for their death, but since he'd been so small, it was only words I was telling him and not that he had much of a bond with them."

"Good for you. I think that's what I would

have done in the same circumstances. I honestly only heard bits and pieces about what had happened over the years. It will be…well, not nice to hear it all, but it will be helpful in getting to the bottom of what is going on now. I'm to understand that you believe that one or more of the men that night has targeted you at your personal home and work?" She told him that was what she'd been told and that she didn't have anything personal anymore but her truck, and that was getting too old for anyone to care about breaking. "If anyone in this room told you that, you might as well take that as gospel. There isn't a better group of people to get to the bottom of things than this group."

When Becka stood next to him, he didn't know what to do. It had been three days since he'd figured out that he was her mate, and it bothered him on so many levels that he'd not told her yet. He knew that it was well past time and stood up. Everyone turned to look at him, but he felt like he was on a mission. And it was to make sure that she didn't find out that he belonged to her from someone else.

Grabbing her hand and nearly dragging her out of the office they were in, he pulled them both into an empty office after trying door after door to find one open. As soon as he found one, nearly weeping when it turned in his hand, he pressed her against the door they'd only just come through. Backing away when she looked afraid, he just said what he should have said to her a few days ago.

"I'm your mate." He wiped his hand over his face, pissed off with himself that he'd just blurted it out there like that. That was when he started pacing. It was time for him to spill his guts as Toby had told him to do before it was too late. Perhaps it was, he thought before speaking again. "I've known for three days now. I didn't know, but Toby told me. I don't know—it's been pointed out to me that I don't know shit about what I am and what I have as an immortal bear friend. Anyway, I want you to know that I have no desire to piss you off. While I more than likely have, it wasn't my intention to do so. Nor to overwhelm you with me. With all you have going on right at the moment, I would think that you'd have enough without me adding to it. But I guess that I fucked that up, didn't I. Oh well. I know that I'd be both pissy and overwhelmed if I was handed all the information that you just got, then on top of that, finding out that you have a mate there too. I'm profoundly sorry for dropping this on you so quickly and all at once, but—" She put her hand over his mouth.

"One thing at a time, if you don't mind. You said that Toby told you three days ago. That means the night that you were at the campsite that we'd stayed at, correct?" He said that it was. "I see. All right. So you knew this information that they were going to dump on me, too."

"No. I didn't. In fact, I wish with all my heart that I'd never done it today, but—again, it was pointed out to me that I'd better tell you before—I didn't have a background check done on you either. That was Launder. She's been looking for a driver to get delivery of items for the charity that she and the other women are working on. I mentioned you, not knowing who you were to me at the time, but I know that you were an upstanding person, according to the people who have used you before. I also let her know that you were mostly armed and you knew how to take care of yourself. Shooting that guy...never mind. They said you'd done a good job with that, too." She nodded but didn't say anything. For the first time in his life, Brad hated the silences and filled them with babble. "I ended up staying the night in my car that night, just down the road from where you and Toby were sleeping. However, I didn't stay there alone. Not with a woman, however. It was Hamish, Launder's mate, and my dearest friend, who popped over to see me. We talked about some of the things that Toby had told me. Not just about you being my mate but other traits that I have that are bear-like. I've never had anyone point them out to me before. Like how my hair is the color of a black bear. Which is what I have been magically enhanced by."

She asked him if he was finished telling her things or simply out of breath. He told her that, for now, it was both. But that didn't mean that things wouldn't come to him again and that he might need to tell her.

"I've known a great many shifters in this line of work. I don't have any trouble with them and having mates. But I will need to talk to you about it at some point. Toby is my nephew, as you know, and I won't have you killing him off to make some sort of statement to the world. Nor will I allow you to treat him any differently than you would a child of your own. He's all I have left of my sister and brother-in-law." Brad told her that he could be honored to treat Toby as he'd been treating him. "Good. I don't know what that means for you, but he is a good kid and comes first in my life over someone I've only just met. No matter what you might think of as being my mate."

"Great." While she paced, he looked around the office that he was in. "This is a lovely office. I love all the bright colors. My office looks like a turd redecorated it. Everything in it is a different shade of brown. Nothing else, no white or even black. Just brown. That's from my secretary. She asks me daily if I'm allergic to color. If I showed her that this is what I wanted, then she'd probably love it a good deal more. I'm not good at arranging. You know? Colors or flowers. I would just stick them in a vase or whatever and be done with it."

"You're babbling again. But my office is the back of my sleeper." He nodded but didn't ask her anything, trying his best to keep his mouth shut so he wouldn't babble like an idiot again. She seemed to be processing things. "They're not going to like the way this story goes. Not any of them. It bothers me to no end how these people met their deaths in the sloth. Is that what you call a group of bears? It was Toby—again who told me what the group was called that he studied at. Why is it really important to them? To find out what happened, I mean? Do you suppose they think that I had something to do with it?"

"No. I can tell you right now that they don't feel that way at all. They really want to get to the bottom of this for you. And now me. Since we're mates, and I'm not trying to force you into anything, but since we're mates, they want to protect you as much as I do. And if this guy is lurking around your home, the truck, then he has to be dealt with sooner rather than later. Before it becomes an issue. And I, along with Hamish, believes that it will. It's been all this time, and he's still sniffing around, which makes me think that he's not finished yet." She asked him if he had any more information for him that she needed right now. "Just this. I'm an ancient. Very old, and with that, I have a great deal of power and magic. Also, we have more money than we could spend in several lifetimes. While I'm not at all sure what you'd want or need, I want you to know that I'm going to bend over backward to give it to you. To be honest with you, I'm excited to have you both in my life. I feel better and more alive than I have in some time. What I have is now yours and Toby's. The magic, too, is yours that I can share with you and Toby. It will not only protect you but also make you immortal. I do believe that you and Toby are that now."

"Too much information right now. Just let me process this and if I have questions — which I'm sure that I will, I'll ask you. But if you don't mind, I'd like to get this over with. I have shit to do, and it's not getting done while I stick around here. Most of it is some of the deliveries that I had to cancel or were canceled for me." She left him there, and he had to laugh.

Well, he thought to himself while wearing a sappy grin that he could feel on his face, she was going to fit right in with the other women in this kiss, and he couldn't wait until the two of them could get some downtime to get to know one another in all ways possible.

When he walked into the room that he'd been in earlier, she'd not started talking yet. As soon as he was seated, as close to her as he could be without crowding her, she started on the story. He knew that she was reliving it just by her tone and her words. It must have been the most difficult thing for her to tell them than anything that he'd seen in all his life. His heart broke for the things that were coming out of her mouth. And for the things, the people that she lost when she'd been sitting for her nephew.

"Liza had a great pregnancy. She wasn't sick at all, and Roman was the most doting husband and father-to-be that I'd ever seen. Just after they had Toby, things started to fall into place for them. They had extra money, and they wanted to spend all their time with Toby. Which was possible for the two of them as they both were able to work from home together. However, they also needed some adult time, a time to be with other adults that were about their age. That night…I was staying at their home because I didn't want to have to drag all the items that went with having an infant in my care to my house."

~*~

The rig that she'd purchased had been delivered to her home that late evening. It had been on backorder when she'd ordered it but had come in about two weeks earlier than planned. She'd been so excited that she'd danced around her sister's living room with Toby and singing at the top of her lungs while doing it.

She called her sister and asked if they minded if she took Toby to the house to see that it was what she had ordered. She didn't really care if it was all wrong; she was going to take it on a long test drive if she could and take her first nephew with her on the ride of their lives. At least, that's all she had planned that night.

"My family was more than happy for me to be able to get on the road. It had been my plan then was to only do it part-time, but things changed for good that night. It was a way for me to make some good money while on the road so that I could take some online classes and make money at the same time. It sort of worked out that way but Toby was the one that was going to school." She let herself think hard about the events that had led to the two of them, herself and Toby, that saved their lives.

"I need to start from the beginning. It's not much more than you already know, but for one thing. Roman's mother lived with the two of them when her husband had passed away not long after they were married, within a couple of weeks, I think." Becka laughed a little when she thought of the faces that Ms. Jermon would make at her when she didn't think anyone was looking. "She wasn't particularly a nice person and hated me on sight. I was fine with that, I didn't much care for her either. She thought that I was a bad influence on the two of them, and I might have been. But they were happy for the most part, and I was going to help them afford to get out of living with the old dirtbag and get a home of their own.

"They lived in a tiny two-bedroom apartment then. Calling it an apartment was really overstating things. It had the two rooms that beds were in, but it was far from large enough for them to have even a dresser in there. The elderly Jermon woman decided that she wasn't going to be giving up anything just because they decided against her advice to have a child. The old bitty not only took over one of the two bedrooms as her own, but she also had her things in the living room that she'd not allow them to touch. She, of course, hated me with a passion simply because I wasn't going to allow her to treat me like she did my sister. Toward the end, just before they were killed, they purchased a house and were going to move in the week following their date night." She thought of how beautiful her sister had looked on the night they were killed. "While they were out and I was on my way toward my home, the sloth was attacked. While I don't understand the full reason for why someone would do that to the entire group, it was made clear that they only wanted to kill the people there and not take over anything. Every person was killed, all the houses were destroyed, and even the pack house, which I'm to understand now, was supposed to be left standing for the next group that might take over. It was not just burnt to the ground, but people — the older and infirmed group had been locked inside before setting it to flame, and they were burnt alive when they found them hiding there."

"They wanted them out of the way so that the land could be sold off and developed into a strip mall and some high rent apartments. But as it turned out in so many other takeovers, the land didn't belong to the man who ordered their deaths, but it reverted to the king when it was no longer considered land for the sloth. That's a new law now that I'm liking, but not in the way that I inherited the land that your family was on. I'm profoundly sorry for your loss, Becka." Calhoun explained how he'd not been the king then, or he might well have been looking deeper into things. "As it turned out, the land and all the houses that had been left standing, even for as damaged as they were, were given to me as king when I took over the position. I'm sorry to have interrupted you."

"No. That's fine. I didn't know that part. That explains why I wasn't able to go on the land to see if there was anything left that I could save for their son." Calhoun nodded. "So, they asked me to babysit Toby, and it ended up being the thing that saved both of our lives. I was thrilled that they were going to have some them time and agreed easily. I was watching Toby at their home when they left to go to dinner. It didn't even stress my sister out all that much while, getting into all kinds of arguments with her mother-in-law. And I didn't mind telling her to shut up when Liza and Roman left, either. However, when I got word that my rig had arrived, I was very happy to get out of the house and leave her to whatever she thought that she needed because I was there. I needed an excuse to get away from the old bitch, and that was perfect. So I asked my sister, and she told me that was a good idea—the two of us had a good laugh when I called her after leaving the house too. It was then that I decided that I was going to keep Toby all night so that they could have some fun. I even sprang for a hotel room for them so that they could be together. We couldn't have been off the phone for more than a few seconds when it started. They were at the house when the door was broken into, and they were...the three of them were taken to the sloth field they had meetings at."

She thought about what she knew and decided not to sugarcoat things. Toby already knew the entire story, so she wasn't worried about him being upset. He would, she knew that, but it wouldn't be a surprise to him what she was going to tell them.

"The group was gathered in the field and tied up everyone that they'd been able to round up—I'm sorry. This is going to be out of sync. I remember it how I was told, and it was so...I think you can understand that it was brutal to even hear what had happened that night. It wasn't a big sloth, only about fifty or so people not counting children. The women, including the old bitty—I didn't care for her at all, but it hurts me deep in my heart whenever I think about how they were brutally murdered. The women were all raped while their families watched. No one was spared. Young or old, they were raped and then killed. While the men watched, they were killed by having their heads bashed in with stones that made it so that they were unrecognizable even with dental records. After they went around the group of children, shooting them once in the head while their fathers watched on, they turned to the men." She thought about what she'd been told. "Their animals were even tied to the back of the cars they'd found keys for and dragged them until either they were so damaged that they again could not be recognized or the rope broke. After piling them all up in a large pile, all the dead, they were burnt, and their bodies were tossed onto the fire pit until there was nothing left of them but a few skeletal remains that made it impossible to tell how many bodies had been there."

Toby got up to leave. She knew that even though he knew what had happened, it still bothered him as it did her the way that his parents were murdered. He hugged her tightly before stepping out of the room. Hamish asked her if he was going to be all right.

"No. Never." She sat down then and was glad that Brad had taken her hand in his hand while she finished the story. "I'd tried to get in touch with my sister the next morning. Getting in the rig with Toby, I made my way to the house. As I was getting closer to their home, I noticed the smoke first, then all the police presence around the area. Instead of stopping, knowing on some level that they were all dead, I made my way out of town and to the first parking lot that I could find to turn on the radio to see if I could get some information."

"It was on the news for weeks. I remember that. I also remember thinking that whoever did that to the group should be treated with the same disdain." Ruby, visibly shaken up by the story, said that she was going to step out and check on Toby. When she left them there, Hamish asked her to continue.

"I didn't return that night nor for a month afterwards. It was difficult to travel with an infant, I didn't know a great deal about babies then, but Toby had been such a good kid that I never had any trouble with him being my sidekick while driving. So, while we were getting to know one another, it became evident that, to me anyway, that by going home, I saved both our lives. And I was going to make sure that I kept on keeping him safe." She looked out the window at the office. She could see Ruby and Toby talking and had to smile. He was so much taller than her that it was comical to her. "No one ever contacted me about Toby. I wasn't notified that my sister had been murdered until a couple of years later. By then, I was traveling full-time. When I was informed of their deaths, no one mentioned Toby and where he might be. I think, like a lot of people did, that he was a part of the mass killings that had occurred."

"How did you get around explaining that you had a child? I mean, some people might have noticed that he was a bear, and you weren't." She told Launder that no one had ever asked, and she didn't explain. "Good for you. I wanted to remind you now that the adoption paperwork has been filed and no one is none the wiser that it's sixteen years too late. He is legally yours now. Toby told me that you had a bit of an issue with him getting into school a couple of times. That should take care of it." She thanked the other woman.

"Sometimes I can go for weeks and not

think about how they must have suffered. Then it will hit me how much...there was no reason for what happened to them. It will take me to the floor when I hurt for them. But I keep telling myself that I got to save Toby. Although it's been hard on both of us, he's alive, and a part of my sister that I might never have gotten if they'd not decided to go out that night. Nor with me going home would I have been able to keep him safe." Calhoun asked her if she thought they'd have killed her, too. "Without a doubt. They were there for one thing, and that was to kill as many people as they could. So far, they've gotten away with it, too. No one has come forward talking to the police—there was no one left, and no one has ever connected me to the next of kin to my sister."

"You think that they thought that you were in the death toll too then." She nodded. "Were there any death records files? For you and Toby?"

"I don't know. I do know that there is insurance that was taken out on the two of them. But I think that when I disappeared too, they just assumed the worst. I was among the dead like— Someone is with Toby and your wife, Mr. Meyer. And from here, it doesn't look like a social...Your wife has it under control."

When she turned to tell them that she'd knocked the man on his ass and had him down, she saw that it was just her and Brad in the room. He had the strangest smile on his face when she asked him where they'd all gone.

"I don't think you finished your sentence before they all just disappeared. I might not have said this to you before, but they're very protective of each other. And that would include you and Toby now." She asked him why he'd order them to protect her and her nephew. "Oh, I didn't. I would have if it had occurred to me, but they see an issue and take care of it. I have no doubt too that soon, if not already, you're going to know who the man is that has been following you around as well as getting any answers that you don't yet have about their murder, too."

They ended up going down to the first floor of the massive building the old-fashioned way. Becka didn't ask if he could do the popping thing and was glad that he didn't suggest it. As she'd been saying before, she was overwhelmed by everything.

Toby was laughing when she got to him.

When he hugged her to him, something he'd done all his life, she put her hand on his chest and asked him if he was all right. He told her that he was better than all right and was looking forward to having dinner with all the people present. She looked at Brad, the first she'd heard of them having dinner together and he said he'd not known either. But he thought that it would be fun. She did, too, but had a lot to do before she went out again.

"The man was making lude comments about my wife hanging out with a younger man. He wasn't believing the fact that Toby was her nephew, so she showed him that he'd better be more polite or she'd show him how. I don't think that he's going to be assuming anything anymore." They all laughed, and Calhoun, what he asked to be called, thanked her for telling him about it. "I'd find out about it, but it wouldn't have been all that big of a deal to her, and it would more than likely have been about six months from now. Not only do we protect each other, but the wives keep us out of trouble as well."

Dinner was loud and friendly. It took both her and Toby a while to get used to the noise. Having only been the two of them for so long, it was as if the volume had been turned up as high as it would go. She figured that when they'd been put into an empty room with the door closed, that this group must do this a great deal. Especially when they could all get together. When her salad was brought to her, she remembered the last time she'd had one and how it had been covered in specks of blood. She looked over at Toby when he was laughing.

"I was just thinking the same thing." The story was related to the table by Brad. Toby was helping him tell the story, and it was louder and longer than she thought was necessary. But she really didn't mind. They were having a good laugh, and sometimes that was all that was needed to bond people. A good story and some fun times.

She'd killed a man while she'd been enjoying her lunch, the first real salad that she'd had in a long time, when a man approached her, thinking that she was Brad's wife and could make him do what they wanted. However, when he tried to muscle her, she killed one of the men and held the second one with a gun to his head. Toby had kept eating his meal, telling her that he'd not had a good home-cooked meal in some time and was going to enjoy it.

After dinner, the lot of them helped the waitstaff clear the table so that they could use it for talking. It wasn't like her nor Toby to be up so late, but she tried her best to hang on. Toby, his body growing by leaps and bounds, was nearly asleep while sitting in one of the many lounges that were throughout the restaurant for people to sit on while awaiting a table. Waking him up, he stood up and looked like he was ready to do battle. Something that he did every time they were out and not in their usual bed. The two of them had to be on the go at all times when they were using a parking lot to sleep in sometimes.

On their way to the rig, Brad asked them if they'd like to stay in a hotel tonight. He just happened to have three rooms, one for each of them, that were connected by connecting doors. She no more believed that he'd just happened to have them, but she was exhausted, and a bed did sound really good.

Toby just looked in her direction when she asked him if that was something that he might enjoy. He told her to have a bed that he could stretch out on sounded like a dream come true.

They decided to stay the night in the hotel. She thought it would be nice to stretch out, too.

Just as she was ready to turn off the lights, Toby asked her if he could talk to her. When she agreed, he came into her room and sat on the floor. The kid was getting taller by the day, she'd swear, just remembering how tall his father had been when he married his mom. But he didn't look like he was in the mood to remember things, and she asked him what he needed from her.

"What do you think of the family? I guess all of the families." She asked him why he was asking her that. "Because it's the first real friends that we've ever had. They are helping you out with some of the million questions that you've had over the years about being a bear and having one in the family. Not to mention, they all seem to be genuinely nice."

"I don't know what I'm to think. To be honest with you. In actuality, I never gave it any thought. Why do you ask? Is there something that I should know?" He asked her what she meant. "They're really nice, but I'm worried that they're only pretending to like me because of you. Also, the fact that—I'm still wondering about that, but because of Brad, supposing to be my mate. I only have their word for it and, of course, yours. I don't know all that many people like you do. I have a very limited pool of information about a great many things concerning you."

"Okay. That's just silly. Why would they only tolerate you to make me happy? I don't know if you realize this or not, but I'm just a small cub in comparison to having the king of my kind – not to mention the king of vampires in the family." She answered him. "Okay but you do realize that, like I said, I'm only a little bear compared to them. If they really were afraid of me attacking them, which I don't see, then I'm reasonably sure that they could each take me out before I was able to shift. I don't want to attack them, but they have more firepower than I will ever have. You're goofy if you think that I'd even contemplate doing something like that. But however, I want to point out that I'd give my life if they hurt you in any way, Mom." Her heart swelled up with the love that she had for this kid. She couldn't have loved him any more than if he'd been her biological son.

She got up to pull the blankets off the bed to join him on the floor. Giving herself a few minutes to get her emotions under control, Becka sat with him. She asked him, point blank, and he'd better be honest with her if he was tired of being on the road all the time. Becka knew or thought that she knew the answer to that. He was sixteen and wanted to drive and meet girls. And that would be difficult to do with his aunt/mom hanging around him because he wasn't yet old enough to drive a big rig.

"Not sick of it. I do enjoy the traveling. And I've seen more of the country than most adults have. It would be nice to have someplace, like this room, to be able to have a couple of days of downtime in." She said he was just thinking about the showers. "That would be my number one complaint about being on the road. The lack of really nice showers. Also, not having to take my gear with me every time I want to get cleaned up. I most assuredly don't like having to share said shower with everyone that wanders in there either." They both laughed. "Are you thinking of giving it up, Mom?"

"Yes. I've been thinking about it for the last several months. I'm not old, but I do not like having to think about hooking and unhooking my trailer. You've been a tremendous help with that, but you'll be off to college soon, and I'm going to have to do it myself again." She smiled at him. "I still remember the first time that you did it on your own."

"Yes, I remember that too. You sent me to someplace and then redid it. I wasn't embarrassed so much as I was a little mad at you about it. Then I thought that you were going to need me, so I decided to have you teach me the ropes so that I could eventually do it on my own. And I ended up being able to do it as well as you did. I'm happy. No, I'm thrilled to have had you as my mother. I don't believe that I would have had the confidence and knowledge that I have about the world without you there with me all the time." She thanked him and wiped the tears away before they fell. "Ah, mom, don't do that. You'll have us both blabbering here in a few minutes, and I need to get some sleep."

When he stood up, he put out his hand to help her up. Instead of letting her go, he hugged her to him and kissed the top of her head. Emotionally overwhelmed, she held onto him tightly as she thought of all the times they'd done this very same thing. Hugged before going to bed for the night.

Chapter 2

Having a few minutes of her own while Toby went with Brad to get some much-needed clothing that he needed, Becka called the insurance company that her attorney had finally tracked down for her. It had been a long time coming, but she'd be glad to have this last detail finished dealing with hers and Toby's family.

"I was going to try to reach you today. As it turns out, there is a birth certificate in Toby's name. I'd swear that it was only just put in the books but for the date on it." Becka thanked Launder under her breath. "Anyway, I have it now, along with the death certificates of his family. Also, a copy of the adoption paperwork has been located as well. Everything that I need is certified, and we're ready to cut the check for the three policies."

"Three? I thought that there was only one, his parents." He told her that since they were all gone, Roman's entire family had been killed that day, too. "Yes, his wife. Oh, I never thought of his mom. It never occurred to me...What are the names on the check going to be? Toby is still a minor, but whatever the amounts are for, he gets it all. I don't want him to have to work going to college. If there is enough for that, I'm going to be thrilled."

"There should be plenty enough for him to get himself a new car as well. The insurance policies have a clause in it that doubles what someone would get in the event of murder. All three of them were murdered. Then there are the homes. Ms. Jermon, Roman's mother, had a house on the land there too. It, too, suffered damage to the point that it had to be torn down, so there is that coming to the young man as well as the house that his parents lived in. It's a goodly sum of money, Ms. Dillard. Close to a million dollars."

"I'm sorry. What did you say?" He laughed and told her that he'd written out the checks today and she could come by and pick them up at any time. "We're not in town yet, but—did you say that there was close to a million dollars?"

"She had a large house, Ms. Jermon did. And there were a lot of valuables in there, too, that she carried extra insurance on. I'm to understand from the man who checked on things for you that everything, including the car, was destroyed. I'm glad to be able to finally put that to rest for you and your young man." Becka said that she was as well. "I bet you are. Also, I'm to make you aware of other things too. The money for the stocks that your family had will be paid monthly after you receive the back pay on the—Ms. Dillard, are you all right?"

"Yes. I am. We've been struggling for a while now, and to know that it's not all been in vain takes a good deal of weight off my shoulders. Toby will be able to do all the things that my sister and Roman wanted him to have. Thank you so much." He told her that she was very welcome and listed some of the other amounts that the checks would cover. Becka only paid about half of attention to it all.

After making arrangements to pick up the checks when they were both in town, she closed her cell phone to think about how Toby was going to be taken care of. She thought that her sister and brother-in-law had done well in keeping their promise to their son that he'd never want for anything.

Crying, she was sitting on the swing on the porch of Hamish's home when Brad joined her. He asked her if he could have a seat with her and was surprised when he sat close to her and took her hand into his larger one.

"I'm getting used to this bear and mate thing. I was talking to Toby about the shoes he wanted, by the way, he wears a size sixteen, when I felt overwhelmed with emotions. He told me that it was you and that you were crying. Toby can feel it, too. Did you know that?" She told Brad that she'd not thought about how much he was feeling her emotions. "I'm sure that you didn't. Why would you? Anyway, is there anything that I can do for you to slay your dragons? I've seen them, you know? Dragons, I mean. I even fought in wars that had me using a sword as well as a gun later. I've seen a lot of things, but I think that the most impressive thing, besides you, of course, is seeing the great beasts up close and personal. There are a few of them in the other realm where Grace and

Allison live."

"Really? Dragons? I guess there are a lot of things that are real that I had no idea of. Griffons. Are they real? I think they're the most magnificent creatures. What with them a part of several animals. And were said to be very powerful too." Brad told her that he'd take her to the castle sometime, and she could see them for herself. "Toby, too. He'll love seeing them. When we were on a long delivery, we would talk about the mythical creatures that we'd have as pets. It was a pretty outlandish list, but it certainly made the drive a lot more tolerable." She looked around. "Where is Toby? You didn't leave him at the store, did you? Can you tell me where he is so that—" He put his hand over her mouth.

"You're upsetting yourself again. Just breathe for me." She did what he asked while still asking after her boy. "He's with Rosie and Ruby at the clinic. They're showing him around and also introducing him to the rest of the staff there. "Toby is just fine. In fact, he is excited about having a pair of boots as well as some summery shoes. I didn't realize how tight things had gotten for the two of you lately."

"Having to get a battery for the rig set us

back a bit. I've had to buy them before, but I'd just put the money down on our vacation. We were going to Disney, the two of us. Well, three of us now, I guess. You'll have to pay for your own ticket, but you can bunk with us in the hotel room. Believe it or not, Toby has been looking forward to the two weeks that we're going to be gone as a way for him to see if he can get a job there during his summer breaks from college." Brad said that he would gladly do that in order to go with them. He told her too that he could pay for the hotel as well. "I have it covered."

"Listen, I might have said this to you before, but I'm a very wealthy man. So what I have is now yours. There isn't any way that we'd be able to spend it all even if we lived a million years. I promise you, we can all go to Disney and afford anything that you or Toby have your hearts set on." She didn't answer him, thinking about the money that she had to pick up yet. She told him about it. He whistled. "That's a good deal of money. I'm betting that you have plans to turn it all over to Toby when he goes to college. And for some reason, I have a feeling that he'd be good with it, too. No overspending unless he needed something really badly. Much like you in that respect."

"I had to cut extras out at the very beginning of the two of us together. First, it was the expense of diapers. He didn't have but a few sleepers to use when he was an infant. No one would see him and that was fine by me. Most of the summer months, he would just wear his diaper to keep cool. Then as he got older, I had to make him aware of the unique way he was growing up and that having the latest fashion just wasn't practical at all for him. But I did buy him things that he needed." Brad told her that Toby said that he had everything that he needed, with the exception of a cell phone. "Yes, I guess so. But he has mine all the time so long as he answered it politely in the event that it was a load we had to carry. But I'll get him one now. He has the money to get himself anything he wants now."

"It's doubtful to me that he'd want anything much more than essentials. You raised him to be a great kid, Becka and it shows well on him." She thanked him and then turned to him again. She needed to clear the air about some things. Becka asked if now was a good time. "Of course it is. And so you're aware, I can't lie to you, not about anything. And I'll never cheat on you either. You are and will be my only love for as long as we wish to live."

"Thank you for that. But what I was going to tell you is that before Toby became a part of my life, I only dated a little bit. I found that I wanted to secede more than I wanted much of anything else. However, since I did have Toby all the time, I didn't date at all. First, there wasn't any way that I was going to leave him as a baby alone while I was out, but even when he was older, I didn't date because, well, for the same reason. This Danny guy, whoever he is, he's out there looking to finish up what he didn't when he massacred the sloth when he did." Brad asked her if she was trying to tell him that she was a lousy lay. Then he laughed. "Laugh it up, big boy, and you'll never find out."

That made him stop laughing but he did pull her to him for a kiss. No pressure, he told her, just that he needed some connection with her before he went crazy. She had noticed that on the other mated adults, they needed to touch one another, or they'd get antsy. She did, however, change the subject then.

"I don't know what your plans are concerning Toby and I but there are a few things that I can tell you now. I'm thinking very hard about not being a trucker for much longer. As soon as a month if I can get out of some standing deliveries that I do." He asked her if it was the one for his place. "Yes, that would be one of them. I have four deliveries that I do in this area and I hate to give them up. But the thought of trying to hook and unhook up doesn't appeal to me as much as it had before. What with Toby going to college soon."

"Excellent idea. That way, I can have you all to myself to get to know you." She glared at him for being much too accepting of her stepping away from her life as a driver. "That didn't come out right. What I meant to say was that I'd not have to figure out a way to get my driving a truck with you. Your partner, I guess. And the thought of settling down, which I've not done much of the last several hundred years, it does have a certain appeal that it didn't before now that I've found you."

"You're saying that you want to stay still from now on? Robin told me that you'd been notified by Hamish to work for him. Does that mean that we'll be living close to them? So, you know, I have no preference as to where I lay my hat. As Toby told me when I spoke to him, it will be wonderful to have a nice solid floor under our feet and a shower that he doesn't have to carry his gear to everything he wants to get cleaned up." Brad laughed, saying he did notice that Toby had left his shaving kit in the bathroom at the hotel even though it was going to be for only one night. "Yes, and towels that we don't have to be hung in the bed of the truck to keep them smelling good. I hadn't realized, or perhaps I'm jaded, that my towels have taken on the odor of diesel since they'd been out so much."

"I did notice that. But I hadn't any idea that it was the towels. Not that it mattered. You were doing the best that you could under the circumstances, and I couldn't be prouder of the two of you." She thanked him and stood up. "I have a load that I have to get in the morning. Then, a round trip to and from a couple of more places. There is a chain that uses me around now that has to get their holiday items early enough for Christmas."

"I'll go with you. I can, can't I? I mean, there will be enough room for the three of us, won't there?" Becka told Brad that Toby had to be dropped off at a local school near the pack to take his tests. "What sort of tests? For driving?"

"School. He can put off the end of semester tests until he gets a few of them finished. Then he goes to a school or college to get his final grades in so that he can move on to the next grade. I don't know what that might mean for him since he's finished with high school as soon as he's finished with his testing. And since he's taking college classes, if he can take more, he has a great head start on his college education thanks to him having a lot of downtime in the truck. However, I think he has his heart set on going to college full-time. To make some friends." He told her how he'd met some of his favorite people while in college. "I think that he will make lasting friendships better if he can settle down. That's another reason for me to want to stop driving. So that he can date and have some friends. We're both sorely lacking in that department."

"I don't have that many friends that I can depend on either. Well, I didn't before meeting up with Hamish and the others. They've been my rock for a long time." Brad stood up when he mentioned dinner. "I'm starving. I just heard from

Toby to gauge how you'd feel about him having a meal with Robin and her family tonight. There are babies there that he wants to get to know."

"I don't care if that's what he wants to do. I feel safer for him there than I would for him to be alone in the truck. Where he does spend a great deal of time in anyway." Brad told her that Toby was going to spend the night and she could pick him up when she got back. She reached out to Toby then as well.

"You have those tests in the morning. Is someone there going to be able to take you to them?" Toby told her how he'd already made arrangements at the pack school to use one of their classrooms for his testing. *"Good. Well, other than you getting yourself something to wear tomorrow morning and tonight, I'll see you when I get back."*

"I got me some clothing while I was out with Brad. I needed some jeans anyway, and they were on clearance with their summer shirts, so I got me a bunch of them for a couple of bucks each. Brad paid for them even though I told him I had money, but he insisted. He kept piling things onto the cart for me. I thought it was for him, but — " Becka cut him off so that he could take a breath and not have a stroke trying to tell

her everything in one breath.

"Toby, it's all right." He let out a long breath that she could almost feel. *"I heard from the insurance company. I'm going to be picking up your money as soon as I get back to the city. If you need anything while I'm gone, just contact me through my cell phone. Brad has one so you can call us with his number."*

"Maybe when you get back, we can see about getting me a phone, too. I can't call you from college if I have your phone with me. I hate to ask that of you but there will be enough money that I can get a few needed things before I go away, right?" She told him that he'd be able to not have to work and get him a car and cell phone before leaving. *"You're not going to just put the money aside for me, Mom, are you? I mean, you've been caring for me my whole life. At least take enough money out of it to get you some things that you need too. Your shoes have more holes on the bottom of them than lace holes."*

She looked down at her shoes. They were the same ones that she'd gotten once when they were out and about right after her sister had died. She supposed if she even were to have paid seventy bucks, a general price of shoes now, she would have gotten a good deal on them. Still, he was right. She did need something that didn't leak snow into her feet while hooking and unhooking the trailer.

After telling him the stops she was going to be doing, she left him to his time visiting. It would be the first of many she knew, her going it alone if she decided to stick with driving. It saddened her to death to think about being alone in the big rig when Toby moved to college.

~*~

While he was glad to see some closure to the trouble that he'd had at one of his favorite places to eat taken care of, Brad didn't appreciate the way that the attorney for the man who had come into his place with the intent to kill his mate handled everything. He'd not known who she was at that time, but he knew it now and wasn't thrilled with the way that she, he had no idea what her name was, had been painting the guy out to be a model citizen.

"Your honor, all Mr. Campsall wanted was for the young lady in question to tell him where her husband was. He had a deal with the man, and it wasn't coming to fruition, and he wanted answers." She showed the picture, not quite getting the dead man in the picture but showing his feet and the blood on the table. "Ms. Dillard not only pulled out a gun when it was simply unnecessary but also shot Mr. Campsall's partner without any provocation."

"What about the gun that I can see right there in the picture in Mr. Campsalls hand? Did he just decide to pretend to be holding it on the young lady?" The woman said that Mr. Campsall had to defend himself. "I see. Well, actually, I don't see it at all. Not your version of it, anyway. Ms. Dawson, have you looked at the surveillance footage that was given to the police? It clearly shows that Ms. Dillard was having lunch with her son and those two idiots, Mr. Campsall and his cousin, what was his name?" She told him. "Yes, Jethro Archer, they approached the young lady in question to pester her. I think that I might have pulled out a gun and shot both of them for interrupting my meal. I've never been to the place in question, but I would love to go there. Isn't that the best-looking fried chicken you've ever seen?"

"It's like my Grannies, Mr. Judge. Best crunch on it that I've ever had." The courtroom laughed when Toby spoke up. "Sorry, sir, but that's the truth. And now that my mom is seeing Mr. Kirk for real, I can eat there when I want. Best place, my mom says, to fill a growing boy."

Everyone that was in the room turned and looked at him when he stood up. Brad cleared his throat before speaking. "Your honor, Ms. Dawson seems to have forgotten that we have both men on surveillance in the back of my factory, reliving themselves in my vats. Not just one of them but all six of them. Making it so that the contents had to be dumped out and the vats cleaned by serializing everything so that we'd not lose any more time than we needed to. If not for Ms. Dillard coming in early, at our request, I would have lost an entire day of work and product going out. That would have put a great many people out of work for several days. And we all know that things are tight all over the world right now. As it was, they had done several million dollars' worth of damage to the cheese factory, not to mention all the overtime pay to have it cleaned up again." Ms. Dawson said that was just a prank on their part. "Prank? Don't you think that they're a little old to be doing pranks, young lady? Not to mention costly ones at that? Sir, I have an itemized accounting of what the damage was in addition to the overtime to clean up the damage that had been too. It comes to well over fifty grand not even including the hazard cleaning of the restaurant, when Ms. Dillard had to defend herself when you presumed that she was the wife of a single man. Even for stupid bad guys, you seem to have your head up your ass." The judge looked at the woman keeping track of the proceedings and asked her to mark that as a fine for him for cursing in his courtroom.

The judge then looked over at Mr. Campsall and asked him about the prank. When he shrugged, for the fourth time since being brought in, the judge admonished him again but not giving a full answer, citing the fact that his stenographer couldn't write that in her comments.

"Like she said, we was just having a bit of fun. Isn't anyone going to be going to jail about killing my cousin, your honor? He's dead on account of her pulling out a gun when we already had things under control and just killed him dead." He was asked if he'd been warned to not point their gun at her that she was armed—it was heard clearly on the surveillance recording that she had warned them several times. Also that she told them, again, several times that she wasn't Mrs. Kirk and had no idea who they were looking for. "Yeah, well, I didn't believe her. Ain't no reason for her to shoot someone just because there was a little bit of misunderstanding. Yeah, that's it. It was all a misunderstanding on her part. That's not right."

"Mr. Campsall, I do believe that I've heard enough. I'm going to send you to jail until you either figure out that the truth will get you finished up sooner rather than later, but mostly, you need to get your facts lined up. Playing pranks, as you called them, are not something that a man your age should be doing, not when it costs someone else a great deal of money." He did some writing before he looked at Campsall again. "You will pay half of the damage done to Mr. Kirk's place of business, then you will do community service until such time that I feel you have paid your debt. Additionally you will reimburse Mr. Kirk for all the cleaning of both the factory as well as the restaurant. The other half of the damages will be paid out of Mr. Archer's estate, if he has one. You will also pay Ms. Dillard a sum of no less than ten thousand dollars for her role in trying to set you straight. Which I will admit that I don't think that's even remotely possible knowing you the way that I have in the last hour or so. Also, I've only known you for a short amount of time. I doubt that you would have learned anything, no matter how it was explained to you that you don't piss in another man's milk. Any questions? Good. Get this man out of my sight."

There wasn't going to be a jury trial for the two men. Even though Mr. Archer was deceased, he would still be held accountable for his role in what had happened. It seemed that everyone was thrilled about the outcome, but for Mr. Campsall and his attorney. She asked him for a moment of his time as he was being hugged by Becka.

"We need to strike a deal, Mr. Kirk. You know as well as I do that if this goes to trial, it's never going to stick. They'll see my client as the victim because he was just playing around. Why don't you name a sum and I'll talk it over with Mr. Campsall. That way, you're not out any time or more money. Because if this goes to trial, you're going to end up paying out the butt for this sham of a trial." He named a sum and smiled. "Let's be reasonable, sir. You have to know that this isn't going to work out for you in the end. The next judge might not be so stubborn about listening to the facts that were right there for him to see."

"And what facts are those, Ms. Dawson? You know what, I don't care what you say. I believe that I will take my chances with a trial. You never know. I might just get more money out of the estate than I expected. Wouldn't that be great?" She told him that he was simply a greedy man. "Perhaps. But if you believe that anyone is going to think that what he did to my factory was a prank, I'm afraid that you're in for a rude awakening. I also think that I'm going to make a call to the law board to find out if you're as good as you think you might be." Turning his back on the other woman, he shook hands with Toby. He felt himself being jerked around by someone grabbing his shoulder. It was all he could do not to reach out to Dawson and tear her throat out. "Unhand me before I tear out your throat, Ms. Dawson. I'm not a man to be fucked with. What do you want?"

"I want you to do what I want. David…Mr. Campsall doesn't deserve to be treated this way. He's a good man and a great father." He asked her if she was his daughter. "Step-daughter. But that makes no difference. He is a good man."

"Good for the two of you, but what was said in this courtroom is what I agree with. Either unhand me, or I will press charges against you as well. You'll find out the hard way that I'm not a man to be messed with." Brad watched the struggle she seemed to be having as it moved across her face. "Whatever you're thinking, you should understand something, I'm not human. You are. How long do you think you'll last against me knowing that."

"I loath you." Brad said that he could live with that. "I'm going to get you, Mr. Kirk. If it's all I do for the rest of my life, I'm going to make you pay for my dad being in prison."

He didn't break eye contact with the woman as he asked the man standing behind her if he'd caught the threat. Even when she was pulled away from him and read her rights, he still stared her down. Brad really wasn't one to fuck with, and she'd soon find that out the hard way if she touched him again.

Once she was in cuffs, he had the jailer pause just for a moment. Smiling at her, he let just enough of himself go so that she could see that even though he wasn't a bear shifter, he was as deadly as one. Perhaps even more so.

"Not only am I going to press charges, I'm going to look into having you disbarred. As I have said to you several times now, you've messed with the wrong person." She told him that she'd see. That she'd be getting out of this, too. "I guess we'll have to wait and see, now won't we. Have a good day, ma'am. I know I will, just knowing that you're off the streets along with your dad."

He was in the sunshine outside the courthouse when he realized that he didn't know how he'd gotten there. Looking to his right, he could see Toby talking quietly while Hamish held onto his arm. He had to peel his fingers away one at a time in order to free himself. Smiling at him, he asked Hamish how long he'd been there.

"Not long. I was worried that one of us was going to pull out a gun. By the way, did you know that Dawson was armed? No carry permit either. Like I have. But she'll be taken to jail over that as well." Brad wrapped his arm over Toby's shoulder before leading Hamish and Toby to the limo that was waiting. "We're going someplace?"

"Dinner. At Toby's favorite place." He heard the boy whoop it up while he was sliding across the seat in the back of the long, sleek car. "My treat. Then we have to go and find us a home that the three of us can live in for the rest of our days. By the way, Toby, in case I forget to tell you again, there is a car at Hamish's home that is for you. I want you to be able to come back and forth from school to see your mom and me as much as you want. All right?"

"Yeah, that's wonderful. Now, all I have to do is learn to drive. And get a permit." He laughed with the younger man. "It's been sort of hectic lately keeping you from being killed, so there's been no time. If you think you can stay out of trouble for a week or two, I might be able to learn a few things that will get me some friends."

"I'll give it my best shot." He decided to hire someone to help Toby out in learning to drive as well as take the written test. It was the least he could do for the boy since he really had been invading his time with work stuff. His mom would be back in the morning if things went well. Otherwise, she'd be back tomorrow afternoon. He was enjoying the time with Toby, and he thought that they were getting along just fine. Even Hamish commented on that. After getting on the road, Hamish showed them the two houses that he'd purchased when he moved here. Toby didn't like either of them and didn't think that his mom would either. She wanted a fenced-in backyard, and he wanted a pool. Time to move on, he thought, and make his beautiful mate glad to give up the open road.

After having some food, the two of them and Toby eating enough for ten men, they headed to the list of houses that Hamish's realtor gave them. It was going to be a long afternoon if all the houses were nothing like he was looking for.

Chapter 3

Marlin looked at the two people that he'd summoned to his office. Actually, they weren't the ones that he wanted, but close enough considering that his attorney was in jail because she'd been armed in a courtroom and his man, his brother-in-law, was dead. All thanks to their stupidity in getting caught with their drawers down, as his grannie had been so fond of saying about him. Tisking, hoping that one of these two would start talking so that he could kill them, his cell phone rang beside him.

It startled him enough that he jumped a little. He'd been so focused on the two men, Lowel and Louis, that he'd forgotten he was waiting on a call. Daring either of them to make a sound, he picked up his phone and said his last name.

"So that's what we should call you is it? Marlin Couch? I think I might have known a Marlin before but no Couches. Why are you harassing me all the time? I don't have time for your bullshit." Hating to be at a loss when he was called, he asked the man who he was. "Brad Kirk. You've sent enough of your people around that you should know my name by heart. I've not even met you, but I can bet that you're a fat fuck who orders people around like he's god or something. What the hell is it you want? I've only just met my mate, and you're keeping me from wooing her the way that I want."

"How did you get this number?" He looked at his own cell and realized that Kirk had called him on his private line. "I don't hand this number out because I don't care to speak to just anyone with a burr up their asses about something that I'm doing. What do *you* want? You'll tell me now, then lose this number. As you might well know, I'm not a man to be trifled with."

"You're men, or I should say your henchmen failed at their attempt to get me put in jail. Also, and I don't know if you're aware of this or not but your pretty attorney isn't going to be able to represent you guys anymore. She's not only been disbarred, but she's also going to be spending a great deal of time—the next thirty or so years at least for carrying a gun into a courtroom without a permit. I'm to understand for also threatening a sitting judge as she was being dragged away. She needs to learn how to keep her voice down when she's calling a judge disparaging names. He has good hearing and heard her calling him a worthless piece of dog shit. Dawson was a good deal more colorful than that, but you get the point. So you tell me whatever it is you want then we'll both go about our lives trying to not interact with each other. What do you say?"

"You have something that I want." Kirk told him that was the way it usually worked out. "All right. I want you to give me some money. A great deal of it, as a matter of fact. Then I'll leave you alone for the moment at least. You have it, and I want it. It'll be easier on you if you simply pay up and shut up."

"That's it? You just want a great deal of money, and you'll what? Poof and be gone? Now, that isn't the way it usually works out. How would you feel if I said no, I'm not giving you money? What would you have to say about that? Perhaps, you should explain to me why it is that you think that I owe you money? I don't think we've ever met, so me owing you is going to go out the window of things that are going to happen." He said that he didn't much care for it and would show him his disdain for it if he were to send someone to him to bring him to his offices. "That's not going to happen either. Option two? If you have one."

"It would be a real shame if something happened to your new family. That young man especially." What Marlin expected was the man to start begging for him to leave his family alone. He hadn't expected to be laughed at. "You don't think that I can do that? Take away half of your new family? Trust me when I tell you, I have ways."

"Oh, I've no doubt about that. You more than likely have a lot of 'ways,' as you put it. But what you don't understand and might as well get used to it, I have backup in my corner, like the man in front of you. I believe his name is Lowel. Would you like to see what I can do to your little operation without even being in the room with you?" He smiled, knowing that the man was full of shit. "All right. Let me know how full of shit you think that I am with this."

Lowel was suddenly headless. If not for him seeing it himself, Marlin would never have believed that it happened. Screaming, trying to get away from the blood, picking random things up off his desk, he tossed not just his cigar box of his favorite cigars but his cell phone and a few other items as well. He thought that it bothered him more that Lowel's body, a fat ugly one at that, was still standing, spraying blood not just all over him but the entire office, too. Screaming, his fear of getting bloodied making him leap back, tumbling over his now failing chair made him knock his head on the safe behind him. Christ, he hated blood. Especially if it was this close to him. If it got on him, like it was now, he freaked the fuck out. Literally freaked out.

Since he had no cell phone on him any longer, he ordered Louis to pick up his phone. When the man looked at him, like he didn't have a first clue on how to even blink, Marlin decided that there wasn't enough decontaminator in the world to make him use his phone ever again. Moving around the mess, difficult to do with blood still pooling under Lowel, Marlin made his way to the front of his secretary's desk.

"Call the police. He killed a man." Dorothy picked up the phone and asked him who had killed who. "That man. Kirk. He killed Lowel, trying to prove some kind of point. Which is…why are you staring at me like that? I said to call the police."

Dorothy asked him the name of the dead man. After telling her, she asked where the killer had come from. The first thing that popped out of his mouth was that he'd been on the phone with him. She put the handle of the phone back in the cradle and stared at him. It wasn't a look that he was particularly happy with, but he asked her what she was doing.

"And tell them what, sir? A man who isn't in your office killed a man over the phone? I never let him in, so I couldn't tell them who the man was nor if he had…how did he kill Lowel? Gun? I haven't any idea. Was he there before I got in? I'll need details if I'm going to make the call. I'm not getting into the middle of things without lots of details that cover my own ass. What do you mean he killed Lowel over the phone? Perhaps we should start there. I might be able to call someone if I have a lot of details. You will, too, if you know what the police are going to say when you tell them that story."

"He just lost his head." Giggling a little, not liking that his mind was suddenly thinking hilarity was in everything that he said, Marlin pressed his hands tightly over his mouth and didn't speak. Starting for his office, he turned on his heel to leave the building. He'd never be able to work in that room again. Not after the massacre, that's what he'd thought it would look like even if he had all the walls and carpet changed out.

Once he was on the streets, he heard phones going off all around him. He didn't like the fact that they were loitering in front of his place of business, answering calls, but he was too busy to mess with them today as he needed to inspect his clothing for any more blood. As it was, one of his— One of the people, a woman that had her cell to her cheek asked him if he was Marlin Couch.

"Yes. Who wants to know?" She handed him her phone and he wasn't sure how to hold it. It had so much crap and glittery stuff all over it that he knew that it had to weigh about three to four times more than it would have had she not decorated the damned thing. "Who is this?"

"It's Brad again. It seems that your other phone got a little messy from my proving to you that I can get to you anytime I wish. And I will if you fuck with me any more than you have so far. By the way. Did you know that blood from a vampire will disappear with any contact with the sun? I didn't either. Not that you have vampire blood on you, there are a couple of spots on your mouth where you should just lick away. However, like I said, vampire blood will simply go away, and then you'd be as pristine as you were before if you're asking. You're a very strange man. Has anyone ever told you that before?" Not to his face, he supposed, but he wasn't going to talk to the man who was…well, he didn't know what he was doing

He looked around, looking for the bastard that had so much detail about him. He had to be close. He knew to have so much detail about the blood that was on his face. While he couldn't find him, not even standing next to him, Marlin pulled out his handkerchief and wiped at his mouth. There were two fat streaks of blood on it. Dropping it to the ground, backing from it, he'd had just about enough of this man's childish games.

"Where the hell are you? I demand that you show yourself, or so help me, Christ, I will end you." The man laughed, no longer using the phone. He could hear the man in his thoughts like he was right there with him. "I'm not fucking around. Show me your face now."

Backing away from the woman, the woman who had handed him her phone who now had the face of Kirk, he hit the back of his head on the wall behind him. Everywhere he looked, there he was. Peoples faces. The reflection in the glass that was the doors to his office. The manhole cover was a larger version of Kirk. He was on fire hydrants, flower blooms, as well as his own face when he looked for an avenue to escape and saw himself again in the reflection.

"Did I do as you wanted? Can you see my face? I should hope you'd know the look of the man that is going to make your life a living hell." The laughter made him feel like he was going insane. It was high pitched and—no. That couldn't be right. It was him screaming not the man that was even now taunting him.

Terrified now that he might well be going

insane, Marlin had witnessed firsthand his mother going over the edge when she'd nearly gunned him down one trick-or-treat night when he'd been about nine.

He'd been dressed as a ghost, a sheet over him with holes cut out for his eyes. It had been all he could afford with his mother driving his father away, and there no money for any food in the house. As it was, Marlin had had to be treated at the hospital when his mother had tried to strangle him using the very sheet that he'd been wearing. After that, he'd gone to live with his grannie, a mean old buzzard that wanted him out of the house so that she could be alone again.

Turning his back to the streets of people that he didn't want to look at, Marlin closed his eyes as tightly as he could. Putting his thumbs in his ears so that he'd not hear anyone screaming — he knew on some level that it was his voice that he heard — however he wanted nothing to do with the crowd that was forming right next to him. They were out to get him, just as his mother had told him when she'd been trapped by the people who had come to take her away.

Marlin didn't know how long he'd stood

there, humming and singing the alphabet over and over, until someone touched his shoulder. Again, something that his mother had done a great deal toward the end of her short but eventful life. Cringing from everything, he begged whoever touched him to leave him alone. He was barely hanging on to his own sanity and didn't want to drag someone else into it.

"My name is Officer James Billing, Mr. Couch. We were called to do a welfare check on you by some of the people in your office to make sure that you're all right. If you don't mind answering a few questions, I can get you some help. You seem to be needing it." He told the man that he wasn't all right. There was a headless horseman in his office. "Headless horseman? Are you telling us that you have a dead body in your offices? I'll have to check that out, of course. Will you be able to stay with my partner? I won't be but a few minutes."

"Yes. That man did it. He has been taunting me for the last few hours. I want you to go arrest him for the murder of my associate." He asked if he was the headless horseman. "Well, of course it is. Are you even paying any attention to the things I'm telling you about? There is a bloody mess in my office that this Kirk guy did it to my associate when I threatened to harm his son. I will, too, but if he's in jail...Will you please just go and see if he's killed anyone else? My secretary is up there, and I'd just as soon she wouldn't be hurt too. She knows a great deal about my operations, and I'd just as soon she was dead than talking up a storm. Go check. He's up there in my office with my other henchman."

They followed him up the elevator without saying a word. He certainly didn't want to see the mess that was in his office, but he'd do this, just this one time, for them. Hopefully, it would take care that Kirk was in jail so that he could get into his office and ruin the man. Marlin couldn't remember right off the top of his head if Kirk had done anything to him, but just the fact that he'd killed someone in his—

"Mr. Couch. You gave me a fright when you ran out of the office a half hour ago. What's the matter? I know that you didn't have any appointments today, but—" He asked if she'd gotten someone in his office to clean up the mess? "The mess? I'm not sure what you're meaning. Mr. Lowel and Mr. Louis are awaiting your return so that they can — what are you doing now?"

He forcibly pulled Hilda from her seat and made her open his door. While she was doing that, he turned to the police officers and told them to just wait. They were going to see what Kirk had done to him. And Lowel. It occurred to him that Hilda had said that his men were waiting to talk to him, but one of them was dead, and he didn't know what to think of —

"Mr. Couch. What dead body are you talking about?" He slipped around the officer who had entered his office. There wasn't a body. "You said that Mr. Kirk removed his head and that he was in here. I don't see anything like you described. The only two men that are in there are your henchmen; you did call them that. But no body — headless horseman or whatever. Are you sure that's what you saw?"

"Yes, I'm sure. It was right there. I had blood all over me. I had to toss my jacket off because it was covered." He picked up his suit jacket by two fingers and handed it off to the man. "Just have a look at that. See that it's covered in blood." It wasn't.

Even when the officer turned the jacket inside

out, it was still as clean as it had been when he put it on this morning. Grabbing his jacket from the man, he tore it into pieces while trying to find even a spot of blood — he remembered his handkerchief. Digging it out of his pocket, he handed it to the man as well.

"Here. Have a look at this. I know that it has blood on it. I saw...well, I saw it as well." He watched as the two officers exchanged looks. He knew just what they were thinking. "I'm not insane. My mother was, and she nearly drove us all...I'm not insane. I know what I saw."

As was the jacket clean, so was his handkerchief. He was tossing his office when it occurred to him that they'd switched out his office. How they'd done it, he hadn't a clue, but that was all he could think that had happened. He asked Hilda what she'd done with his office. Even to his own ears, it sounded...off.

"Tell me, damn it." He took a deep breath and let it out slowly. He could tell by the look on her face that she wasn't happy with him right now. "Please. I won't be mad. Tell me what you did with switching out my office. And then tell the police that it was all a joke on me. I won't be mad, but I need to know where my office is now."

"It's right there. Where you left it. Are you feeling all right, Mr. Couch? You don't look so well." He started to scream, barely able to hold it back while he tried to reason with Hilda once again about his office. "I don't know what you think I am, sir, but I won't have you accusing me of taking anything out of your office, much less the whole lot of rooms you have. I think you need to let these men take you to the hospital. You're not acting right in the head."

"My head is perfectly fine." Both the officers put their hands on their guns when he screamed. Taking in another deep breath, he did that three more times before he thought that he could speak. "I'm perfectly fine. My head is fine, too. I'm just missing my office. The headless guy, well, he wasn't headless, but he made one of my men headless, and that was all I could think about. You'll see. As soon as someone tells me how they switched the offices around...maybe we're on the wrong floor. That's it. We got off on the wrong floor, and they're playing with my head."

Now that he was saying it out loud, he realized how ridiculous he sounded. Trying to regain some control over…well, everything that he'd said and done today, he looked at the officers and told them without resorting to hysterics that he was all right now. He'd been….he'd been upset before, but he was better now. Trying to back them out of the office, whomever it belonged to, they weren't having any of it. He just knew that he was going to end up in the loony bin like his mother had.

~*~

Brad had to laugh at everything he thought of Couch trying to get away from what he had thought was gallons of blood. There had been nothing there, not even the two men that he'd summoned to his office. It was just Launder having a lot of fun messing with the man's mind. Thinking about how he'd tossed his cell phone at the wall had him laughing all over again. It wasn't until Toby came into the room that he thought he might have some control over his humor.

"You looked weird." That's all it took to set him off again. Leaning on the table so that he'd not fall over, he tried his best to explain what had gone down to Toby while he'd been taking his tests. "No, I'm pretty sure that you're weird on top of being weirded out. Why did he think that there was blood all over him?"

"A trick of the mind." He nodded, but Brad was almost as positive as he'd ever been that the young kid was humoring him. Finally able to stand up without breaking down again, it was Hamish who explained what had happened. While he wasn't laughing as hard as he'd been, Toby finally understood.

"So you messed with his mind into thinking that's what he was seeing. I can do that. I don't get to practice much, but I can make people do what I want them to do sometimes. Mom thinks it's not fair to do that to anyone, but we did use it when someone was getting frisky with her." That sobered him right up. Asking Toby if he knew the names of the men who'd gotten frisky with his mom had him shaking his head. "I don't think so. I know a few shifters, and there aren't any of them that wouldn't use that name and kill the other man. I understand that everyone is possessive, so no, nope, no way am I going to tell you so that I feel responsible for the harm that might come to them." Brad told him that he'd only mess them up a little bit.

Toby snorted. Something that he noticed a lot of them did in this kiss. Even the dog, Joey, was a snorter. Thinking that he could wear Toby down more later, he let it go, at least until his mom returned. He'd figure it out.

As they were going over some of the amenities that were in the three houses that they were going to look at this evening, Toby was telling his mom on his new cell phone how the testing had gone. Toby felt all right about them, he told her.

Toby had been taking his tests yesterday to finish up his high school classes when it was suggested by the leap leader for him to take some tests on life skills that might get him out of a few freshman classes. He had already taken a few of the classes while waiting for his tests to be given to him. He was told that it wouldn't be any trouble for them to test him on his Pre-college courses while he was there. After calling Becka and getting her permission to do it, Brad had dropped the young man off this morning to finish up. Now, they were making plans to go house hunting again, and this time with Becka. They were using the camera on both the phones to look at the houses that were on their list for tonight.

She was holed up at a hotel, waiting to be called from the company that she was picking up one of the orders that she was bringing back for his stores. It was the perfect time, he thought, to see what sort of places that she'd like so she'd be able to look and not take her eyes off the road for any length of time.

The white picket fence and the pool were something that she really wanted, and it seemed that the house they were looking for ticked off a few of the items that she thought needed to be in her home. Oh, and a fenced-in backyard. There wasn't much else he could get out of her, but that she also wanted stability under her feet.

Toby didn't care for the first house. Brad wasn't sure that he did either. It was...for lack of a better term, it was blocky. Like someone had taken discarded blocks of all sizes and stacked them up like they were playing at building a house. The windows even looked like they had been discarded from another house and put in this one to fill in where the blocks wouldn't fit. It was marked off before they even walked inside. The second one didn't fair much better. But when they got to the third home, Brad was thinking that they'd found the perfect home.

While he and Toby toured the house with the realtor, Becka was asking questions that were answered by the other woman. Finding the pool out back, with a slide and rock garden by the pool, he knew that Toby loved it, and so did Becka. There was even a little boat house at the back of the land where they could put his boat in the water and cruise up and down the river. He had a thought that he wanted to get a pontoon boat now instead of something that would be fast. Taking an easy stroll down the river had an appeal that it didn't have for him before. While Toby, much to the amusement of the realtor, swam in the pool to cool off, he walked into the back of the house that was the kitchen.

"The kitchen has been updated in the last year. Both of the previous owners loved to entertain, and doing so in the kitchen was something that they favored. If you'll notice, that kitchen can open up and spill right into the deck with the pool. There is plenty of room in the dining room as well if the weather doesn't cooperate."

While the realtor talked about the tile on the floor as well as the floor-to-ceiling sliding doors, he looked at the craftmanship of the oak cabinets as well as the stone flooring that seemed to him had been dug right out of the earth and smoothed out to make the floor just about as beautiful as he'd ever seen. They were looking at the bedrooms on the second floor when Toby joined him. The kid looked like he'd found his forever home in this place, too.

"I was wondering at the price. It says here that the home has been empty since a year ago. If you're saying that it's priced to sell, why haven't you sold it yet?" He thought that Becka made a good point, but he was willing to pay what they wanted for the house right now. The realtor told them both that it ended in a nasty divorce, and both sides didn't want to give up their part of the home until the judge ordered it. "So we should expect trouble then. I thought things were just too good to be true about this place."

He listened with Becka on what the court ordered sale of the house meant for the two of them as their realtor laid out the particulars. The house had to be sold and there wasn't a reserve on the place. Meaning that if the judge wanted to and someone offered ten cents for the home, and he took it, the money would be divided in half for each of the previous owners. He liked the sound of that.

"What was the last bid on the house?" He wasn't sure that the woman was going to answer Toby when he'd asked. When she finally did, he could have kissed the kid on his mouth. "What do you mean, people just expect it to be expensive. I think a lot of things are expensive that some people don't. Can you just tell me what they want, and we can tell you yes or no? You're not being very helpful that—or is that your plan? Not to sell the house to us?"

"Good heavens, no. I didn't mean to… no, I just didn't want you to walk away from this deal of a lifetime." It was then that Brad realized that Toby had learned how to dicker with pricing from his mom. He just stood there with his hands over his chest like he'd seen Becka do a thousand times in the last couple of weeks. "What I meant to say was. The house isn't cheaply made, nor is it—"

"So you're thinking that because of the way…what? How we're dressed? That my mom is a trucker that we can't afford a home like this one? You've already written us off as buyers? Tell us why you're acting like this if that's not what's going on." The compulsion was there. The only other person that he knew of who could use it that well was Hamish. Brad watched the woman struggle with the words she didn't want to say. Adding his own compulsion, he finally was able to break her down and start talking.

"The primary realtor, my boss, told me not to sell it to anyone that came in. He was waiting for his daughter to decide if she wanted the house or not before he allows anyone to see this place." She looked defeated before continuing. "If anyone else buys this house, even if it's his daughter, I don't get any commission because he's only allowing me to show the house to keep people off his back. Meaning the previous owners and the courthouse. If I were you, I'd call them directly and talk to them about buying it. There is no court order for them, as I was told to tell you, and frankly, they're getting pissy because it's been on the market for over a year, and they want to get on with their lives. I don't blame them, and Shaw is blaming it on the market. Mr. Shaw, Caroll Shaw of Shaw and Shaw Realtor, is holding out for his child. Which isn't a nice thing to do. Here is their number."

Toby was talking to the realtor while he called the Webster couple. They weren't getting a divorce, nor as he was told, were they ordered to sell the place, as he'd only just found out. After telling them what was going on, Becka told them about how the young woman who had been showing them the house wasn't going to be making any money off the sale either. That, he thought, was the worst way to treat an employee of all.

"I tell you what. I'm going to hire you to work real estate deals for my company. I won't shortchange you either. You help me out, and I'll help you. But I want honesty from now on. Not half-truths that will get us both into trouble." He explained how he was forever getting behind in his work because he had to go out and about trying to put businesses in the right building.

Brad told her how he liked to use existing buildings when he could. It saved both time and money for everyone. Benefiting a great many people, too. When Becka said that she was finished with the call to the Webster couple, it was Toby who was smiling. The kid, Christ, he loved this kid already.

"All right. This is the plan. You're going to

sell us the house because we called the Websters as they're good friends of ours. By the way, they're pissed off that Mr. Shaw is doing them dirty. They know that it's in no way your fault, and they wanted to thank you, Rosemary, for telling her when you did. You tell the little fucker that you couldn't very well tell us that lie because we would just check with the owners." Rosemary smiled and asked how much they were going to offer on the house. "Oh, that's been settled, and you will get a commission check on the full amount. For helping them out, the Websters are selling us the home at a great discount because she is planning to get the rest from Mr. Shaw. I have a feeling he's not going to know what hit him. They're pissed off something terrible."

Everyone was in a good mood when Rosemary turned the keys over to them. After making sure that she had her story right about what to tell Shaw, she left them to walk around their new home. Shaw was either going to fire her, which she believed that he might, and she'd welcome it, or keep her commission check. Or try to anyway. That was part of the plan that the Websters were going to care for. Making sure that

Rosemary got what she had coming to her.

Vicki Webster told him there was a boat in the boat house that he could keep because they'd purchased them a much larger one to go deep sea fishing. There wasn't much of that around here, Vicki told him. After inviting them to come and see them when they were in town again, Brad made arrangements to have the things that he had in storage brought to their new home. Their home. He thought that had a perfect ring to it.

"I don't have anything for my room. Not unless you're planning for me to live in the rig from now on." He'd not thought of that when Brad suggested that they stay in the house tonight. Toby had basically grown up in a rig and wouldn't even have a desk that he would be able to use in the house. "I don't even have an air mattress or a good pillow. I never, well, I had hopes of being in a house, but not this soon. Do you think we can hit a couple of shops so that I can sleep in my room?"

"All right. It's shopping time. I own a few furniture stores so we'll hit them up to see what we can get delivered for you tonight. It doesn't have to be anything that you want to keep forever. Whatever we end up getting can go into one of the spare bedrooms. But we'll cross that bridge when we come to it." Brad rubbed his hands together. "Then tomorrow we'll do some shopping to get the things that we're going to need forever. Towels, linens, and the like. Even a couple of televisions now that we can have them hooked up. Do you like sports, Toby?"

For the first time in a very long time, he was excited to have enough money to spend on his new family. Not just a few thousand bucks that he couldn't live without but billions and billions of dollars that were earning him more every day while it sat in his investments. Thinking about all the things that they needed, he decided that he didn't want the things at his home here in his new place with his family; he wanted everything new so that he could make their memories while breaking things in. Mentally rubbing his hands together again, the first thing that he was going to get was an engagement ring for his wife. He wanted to get something for his son, too, to make sure that he knew that he would love him as his own, just like Becka did towards him.

Yes, Brad thought. He was as excited as he'd ever been in starting a new life. From this day on, it was about making his little family happy and safe. And that, in turn, would make him happy. Happier than he'd been in forever.

Chapter 4

Being frustrated wasn't helping either of them. Becka knew that. First of all, she was bored to death, and secondly, she didn't have anything to do. Yes, her head told her they were the same thing, but they weren't. Being bored meant that her mind was inactive—to her at least and not having anything to do, even if it wasn't something that totally occupied her mind, was making her think about things that she didn't need to be pondering about, such as the very fact that she married a complete stranger without any thought of what they'd do with their life together. Like now, she told herself. No thought.

Should it matter that they were mates? She didn't think so. While she'd enjoyed her working life, not going out on dates and so forth, she at least had her job. Now, thanks to people finding out that she was married, she didn't have one. No one wanted to take on a married woman because of how hard the work was for a woman if she were to get pregnant. Why, she asked herself. How did that make one iota of difference than before? Stupid people. She'd lost three jobs just this morning, and it was making her pissy with everyone around her.

When she realized that she was ruining the flowers in the little garden that she'd been sitting in, Becka put her hands on her lap and counted to ten. That didn't have the desired effect, so she counted two more times to ten before getting up and stomping away. She was leaning against the tree sobbing when a faerie found her.

She'd been told several times that she was to get one. Why? No one had an answer other than she should have one to keep her safe. She'd not found the need to have one flittering about her, so she had done nothing to have one hanging around her. Becka knew that wasn't fair of her. They needed a job, too. And this was the funniest thing. She'd never seen any of them *flittering*.

But now that she was bored…pissed off, she

was making everything out to be a hardship on her. When she turned on the little person again, she knew she wasn't being fair. She asked him what he wanted. The little creature flew back from her so quickly that she was sure that it was terrified of her. That hurt her soul that she'd made such a little — it had been like she'd yelled at a baby, and it was puckering its lips, ready to cry.

"My lady?" She asked him what he wanted, then pointed out that her name was Becka. "Yes... Becka. I have come to see if there is anything that I can help you with. I have asked the others to take care of the garden for you."

"Why?" The little man said that it had been torn up. "Yes. So? I did it. Maybe that's the way that I want it to be? Messy." She was being unfair. Unreasonable, too, but she didn't care right now. Or she did care and wasn't ready to let it go. Her heart and head were having a bad day, she told herself. "I'm not even sorry about it. Not one bit. So you tell him to leave it alone."

Why? She couldn't imagine why she'd say anything like that to anyone. And the garden was a mess. So bad that she was sure that none of the little plants could be saved. That hurt her, too.

Knowing that she'd needless killed them because she was…well, she supposed she was a lot lonely. And bored.

Instead of arguing with her, he just disappeared. He might well have flown away; she'd been pointing to the garden and wasn't looking at it when it was just gone. Just as she was going to throw a full-out temper tantrum, someone appeared in his place. A very beautifully dressed woman who seemed to sparkle. Actually, it did sparkle, but Becka lifted her chin and asked her what she wanted. It occurred to her that she was being rude, but she just didn't have the heart to be nice. Or how to be nice to someone that could pop in and out of situations like—she asked it what it wanted.

"I'm not sure that we've been introduced. If we have, then you'd know better than to take that tone, any tone with me. My name is Allison. I'm the queen of faeries. While I don't know you all that well, I want you to know that I won't tolerate you treating my kind the way you have just now. What is your problem? You have to have one because there is no way from what I know of you that you'd treat a small creature the way that you have just now." Becka tried to control her anger, but all she did was stand there with tears filling her eyes and stare at the woman. "I see. So, something is bothering you, and you just took it out on the little people. You broke his heart just so you know that. And for what reason? I demand answers, not tears."

"I don't know." Dropping to her knees, Becka let all the anger, hurt, and pain that had been building up inside of her form into tears and allowed them to just flow down her cheeks, much like the words did that she had no control over. Saying everything that was wrong with her, the loneliness, anger, boredom, and anything else that seemed to have taken its toll on her out on the woman that was in front of her. When she had cried for about thirty minutes, repeating over and over how everything was against her, she laid down on the soft grass and closed her eyes.

"If you wish to kill me off, go on and do it. I don't even care anymore." The shadow of the woman rolled over her, but she didn't look at her. Becka was too busy feeling sorry for herself right now to care about what had happened to her. "This sitting around waiting for someone to knock me around is making me insane. Either do it or leave me the hell alone. I'm about as useless as it comes around here."

"Are you finished feeling sorry for yourself?" She didn't move, said not a word either. "Get up. I hate when someone bows down before me and I hate it even worse when someone is being pitiful. Get up, please, so that we can have a conversation."

She did get up, but she didn't bother with wiping the dirt off her clothing. Lifting her chin up again, it was pushed down by the other woman when she started sprinkling something on her. It felt like rain, but in a few seconds, she realized that she was cleaned up and someplace different. Looking around, she asked her what right she had to take her away from her home.

"I have whatever rights I want. Now, hush up and have a cup of tea with me. I've been where you are before." The woman started asking for things like tea and crumpets. If asked, Becka would have thought that was a made-up name. "It's not made up. They're as real as scones. Now, have a seat there. Oh. You need to have something else on. Something tea having like. And yes, I just made that up."

Becka found herself in a very springy dress. It was covered in daisies and roses, little pink ones. When she put her hand to her hair, and feeling now for the ponytail that she was forever pulling it up in, she found that it was up in a do and had flowers in it too. She told the woman that it was too much. After agreeing, her hair was let down, and she sat in one of the three chairs around the table. She had no idea why but Becka did feel better dressed up the way that she was.

"My sister is going to join us for tea. If you can keep your temper at bay, she might stay long enough to talk to you. However, you being especially rude today might have everyone backing off." Becka felt her face heat up and told her that she was sorry. "As I said, I've been there before. Bored out of your ever-loving mind and no one to complain about it to. At least no one to listen anyway. Yes, I think everyone has. Tell me what it is that has you at odds with yourself."

"I can't work anymore." Allison told her that wasn't it. "It is too it. Why is everyone trying to—" Cocking a pretty brow at her, Becka asked her what was wrong then. "If you know so much, then you tell me why I feel like I'm...at odds all the time."

"You need sex. Actually, I would have suggested that first off, but you seemed to want to pick a fight with me. Anyone, I guess. Poor Andrew is still at the castle sobbing about how he'd disappointed you. They never think that it's anyone but themselves that is at fault. Just so you know, I don't fight fairly. I have a powerful amount of magic, and I'm not afraid to use it on you. No, it's sex. You and Brad need to get yourself's laid, and that'll take care of the two of you in being rude to everyone." She said that Brad wasn't being rude. "Not to you, no. But his friends are avoiding him because he seems to want to get the snot knocked out of him for no other reason than because he's bored, too. I would have thought that it would have occurred to you that you needed to be laid, but I've done a little walk through your head, and there is no point in your life that you ever used sex to relax. Why is that?" Embarrassed again, she didn't have an answer. "I know the reason. It's because you've been the best mother in the world to that young man of yours, and nothing else mattered but keeping him safe. I don't know if you know this or not, but he's a growing man and can and will be able to care for himself if you were to ask him to. Send him over here if you wish. He, unlike you, gets along with everyone around him."

"I'm sorry." Allison sipped her tea and told her that was a start. "Are you going to pick at me too?"

"No. I might well slap you around if you don't tone it down. You're lucky that it's me that got to talk to you and not my sister. Who is meaner than I am when you mess with her faeries." After the other woman showed up, her name was Sarah, she found out, the two of them spoke about the things that were going on around their realm. Becka found herself watching the faeries and other creatures as they worked around the room. She spoke to them too off and on, giving them suggestions about the work they were doing. For whatever reason, Becka found herself relaxing in a way that she'd never been able to do before.

Waking up, she was surprised to find herself in bed with Brad. He was still lying there with his eyes closed, but she wasn't sure if he was sleeping. Sliding out of the bed, careful not to move him around too much, she made her way to the window seat and watched the animals in the yard as they played around.

The place was bright with sunlight and colors. Not just colors a person would find in a crayon box but brilliant colors that defied description. To say that things were red and pink would have been an understatement. She found herself smiling as she mentally made up names for the colors that were surrounding her.

Sighting a dragon, Becka thought that it wasn't real. When he summoned her to come to him, she moved out of the door and to where the big animal was lying in the grass. Like the colors, the size of the creature was more than she could have said. Giving herself only the head of him to compare herself to, she sat down next to him.

The faeries were all over his body and flew away as one when she sat down next to him. For whatever reason, she wasn't afraid of the large animal. Not even when it yawned when she sat down. His teeth, she noticed, were bigger than she was tall and wider than she was at standing up. Christ. After a few minutes, not only did the faeries return, but they also brought her a large glass of juice that she enjoyed immensely.

"You are new to this area. The mate of young

Brad." She said that she was but didn't know how young he was. "Nay, he'd not tell you. But I am older than the young man is. By a great deal, as it turns out. Not that it matters. I do believe that you're the most beautiful woman that I've seen around here. Excluding, of course, my own mate."

"I guess she's around here someplace too?" He told her that she was, heartbrokenly, no longer alive. Humans had taken her life long ago. "I'm so sorry, sir. The only family that I have left is Toby, my nephew. He's only just turned sixteen years old."

"What about Bradley? Is he not your mate and family, too? Even the kiss that you now belong to is your family. Or so I've been told. You aren't alone, ever, my dear. Remember that, if you please." She didn't know how to answer that, so she didn't. "Feeling a bit out of sorts about that, I heard. Or is it something else that has you here?"

"I don't know why I'm here. I guess I could ask, but I've been enjoying seeing things that I've never known were real before that I didn't want to be sent home. Do you suppose that I was sent here because, as you pointed out, I'm being out of sorts?" He laughed, the ground rumbling under his big body. "I would think that if you were to do that all the time, the ground would give up the trees and just have them lying about. How long have you lived here, sir?"

"My name is Adam. And I have lived here since I had no more use in the other land. Humans no longer believe in one such as myself, and that makes my magic hard to keep up with me. Without it, I can no longer fly to darken the sky. No one to ride upon my back either. The saddle that was there has long since rotted away. Nothing, it seems to me, stays as long as one wishes, but now I have a new friend in you. But here, it is like I've been given a renewal in life, and I find that I am enjoying my final days here more than I thought that I might." He sounded so sad about that Becka decided to hug him. Once she was seated, he pointed out that she had a small wound on her hand. "You must allow me to close that wound for you, my dear. Otherwise, you might well bleed out. A small cut from one such as myself could cause you great harm no matter the size of it. Come, let me heal it for you so that I will not worry."

She put her hand out and laughed when he licked her entire body with his massive tongue.

The wound did seal, but Becka was soaking wet as well. Laughing, she shared what had happened with Brad when he came to join them. While Brad and Adam reminisced about old times, she leaned back against the large dragon and watched all the faeries and brownies she was told they were called as they brought flowers and other greens to the big creature. And he, in turn, would politely put out his tongue when they'd gathered enough and eat the things like they were ambrosia to him. Becka thought that it was to him. She'd found scents that she'd never encountered before and figured that it would taste that way, too.

Wondering at what he said about it being his final days, hoping that he only meant in the other realm, Becka knew that she'd come to spend time with him as much as she could. She surely hoped that he'd welcome her back. Becka thought that Toby would enjoy just sitting around talking to him as much as she did.

"Becka?" She looked up when her name was said. It was Allison. "You seem relaxed now. Good. I have some things that I'd like to show you. If you don't mind."

They were walking away from Brad and

Adam when she realized that they were going away from the castle as well. Asking Allison where they were going, she told her that it was a surprise. Not that she cared all the much for surprises, Becka reframed from saying anything that might get her into hot water again. She was happy to see that she was being smiled at rather than treated like she was a bad person. But she did think about the sex that Allison had been talking about.

Sex wasn't anything that she made a big deal about even before she'd taken Toby under her arms. There were plenty of men around, most of them not knowing about her having the little boy who would have taken her out and had sex with her. But that would have been all that it was. Just sex and nothing romantic. She found that she really wanted romance. Being wooed, too. Smiling to herself, she did have to wonder what Brad would think about what was on her mind. Then Allison spoke, bringing her out of thoughts.

"You do know that Brad spent a great deal of time here when he was healing? It had been long ago, but I remember it like it was yesterday." Becka said that she'd not realized that he'd been hurt. "Oh, that's right. Sometimes, I forget that the two of you haven't known each other all that long. To be honest with you, Becka, you two act and hang around one another like a very well-established couple. Decades and decades of loving one another along with being as happy — I would think that you'll get there eventually after having a wild night of sex, I guess. I would have thought had I known differently that you have been together for decades instead of just weeks. I wonder if that has anything to do with the fact that we're all surprised that you don't seem to want to be together."

"I don't know him." Allison said that she understood that now. "So you've been busting my chops over being angry because you forgot that we've not been together? That doesn't seem all that fair of you."

"You're right. It hasn't been. And I'm sorry for that." She said that her sister had busted her chops about her being nosy, too. "I haven't been in the best of moods. I'll agree with that. And you were right to point it out to me. I don't know any of you all that well, so I'm not entirely sure how to make myself be a part of the group. Not yet, anyway."

"You must get over that. Anyway, here you go." She looked at the smallish house and saw that while it was tiny compared to the castle, she thought it was bigger than the house that they were living in with the humans. Becka wasn't sure how to call it anything else. "He designed this place while he was here recuperating, as I said before, and the faeries had the most wonderful time making sure that it was just how he thought it should be. He was hurt badly and wasn't thought to survive during one of the times that he was fighting for the castle of Murry. He and the others, Hamish and all his friends, weren't all that old when they... well, not too old compared to how old they are now. But they defended the castle and won the day by fighting as a team. A concept that wasn't thought of as working long ago. Most of the time, back then, there was no teamwork and that is why a great many of the great families castles were left to ruin. This house, a mini castle you can call it, is a replica of the one in which Brad was injured. He fell from one of the turrets in what would have been his death if not for the dragons of the time. Brad was...I believe you might know this already, a great man and a good friend to all that came to him. Just as you have done for the faeries today. I knew that you'd be perfect for the job. Anyway, the dragon that day, Adam's mate, as it turned out, was happy to have him with her when she perished. So was Adam. He took her dying wish to the other dragon so that he'd not give up his life but tell the stories of their kind to others like himself."

"I'll have to have him tell me the story. But what did you mean about a job? I didn't do anything to the faeries here. Nor would I. They're special and—I guess I did guide them a little when they seemed at odds as to... I didn't do anything bad, did I?" She walked around the larger than it looked mini castle and was amazed at the sheer size of it. Becka would swear that it got bigger as she walked around it, and Allison told her that she was correct. "Why is that? And I'm still hoping for an answer on what I did for the faeries. I don't want to cause any of them any trouble. Ever."

"It...via magic knows that you are the mate to its owner. If you were to step inside, you'd notice things that you wouldn't have if you'd been in before, knowing that you were his mate. The rooms—I guess through their own magic, I would say they're trying to impress you. What do you think? Have they done so? And no, my child, you did nothing wrong with guiding the faeries. You did myself and my sister a great service by guiding them, as you called it." She smiled at Allison and said that she was very impressed. Then she thanked her for not being upset with her. "If you would like to go inside, I'm sure that it will, by one of the faeries that live inside, tell you everything that you would want to know. More than likely a bit more exaggerated than Brad would tell you." They both laughed.

She didn't go inside but did walk around the realm with Allison, telling her about all the things that, because of Brad, were now thriving in this world. Allison told her how he'd been helpful in the waterways that now kept water flowing to the orchard. The large lake that had been resized in order to accommodate the large ships that brought supplies from other worlds. Becka asked how many other worlds there were, fascinated by that.

"Oh my. Let me think a moment. Millions. For every kind of creature there is a realm that their queen lives in. For this one, there are two of us that share this realm because it is so much larger than any of the other realms that are around. This one is the only one too that shares an opening with the one that you're in. Not that they couldn't go between yours and theirs, but it is frowned upon a little. Just because of the difference in theirs and your cultures. You see, my child, my sister, and I were born twins, Sarah older than me. From the first time we started working, we knew that we worked better together rather than apart. That being so, it was also better for us, being a richer realm for us to be able to help out the other places that we visit with the supplies that we get from the human world."

Having as much fun as she'd ever had, Becka asked questions about things that she'd found, and Allison seemed to be proud of her doing so. As they were headed back to the castle, Allison's castle, she saw that Brad was still talking to Adam, and the two of them seemed to be having a grand time.

"He will have had Brad tell the stories over and over again about his mate. I'm sure that Brad has a good many of them, too, as he'd spent a lot of time with her. She fondly called Brad her human child. He and Adam's mate were very good friends indeed. It's good for him. Adam needs someone to remind him that he had made a promise not to perish so long as there were creatures asking about the dragons."

~*~

Brad hadn't had dinner in the castle in a good long time. He forgot, because of the time that he'd been gone, how much he had enjoyed it. He'd often said to anyone who would listen that he'd stay here for the rest of his days if he could. Feeling that even more than before, he wished that he and Becka were able to just never go to the human realm ever again.

If not for the house that they had only just picked out, he would have begged to live here. However, with a new family, he knew that he'd have to ask them what they wanted to do. He'd seen Becka around and knew that she was happy here, but would she want to live here forever? Brad would need to speak to her and Toby about visiting more often.

Not that he didn't love the people who were his friends in the other realm, but to him, this place was so much more relaxing than the one where he'd been born to. Also, he felt as if he could say what was on his mind when he had an opinion. Not to mention the magical beasts and creatures that he so loved to talk to every day.

"Why is that?" He asked Becka what she meant after she hugged him in greeting when he found her on the castle lawns. "I don't know if you realize this or not, but when you're thinking hard, as you were just now, I can feel your emotions as well as hear your thoughts. I don't have to try and read your mind, but I can hear your thoughts like they're my own. So why would you live here full-time? Not that I'm thinking that's a bad idea, I love it here. And think too that you have the right idea about where we should live. Do you think that it's a possibility? It's all new to me and not you. Why would this place be better to live than anywhere else?"

"That is the reason right there. It's always new to me. Every time I come here, I see something that I've never seen before. A pretty flower. A vine growing up one of the large trees that wasn't there the last time. Or if it was, it was smaller than before or didn't have any blooms on it as it did now. It really does seem to change from day to day around here." She told him how much she enjoyed the way things just went on without notice to her or anyone else. "That's a good point. Yes, I can see that. The lands don't try to show off what it's up to at any given time. It just continues to do its job regardless of who might be able to see it working. I like that. Thanks. I've never been able to put it into words like that before." He kissed her on the forehead, thinking that she smelled of the land here, not in a bad way but like the flowers and air. It was the most refreshing thing he'd smelled, Brad realized.

"If not for Toby, I think that I could live here too. I'd want to have a place for him to live here and in the human world if that was possible. He said that he loves it here but would miss the nonmagical aspect of the human world. Then he pointed out how there is more than likely more magic over there than here. I might well have believed him, but I've spent the day walking around and talking with the other creatures here that aren't in the other world. Adam has become a good friend of mine, and I think I could get used to being around him a great deal." Brad thought that Toby had it right about both realms. "I heard that you recuperated here for a time. Was it bad?"

"Not until I regained consciousness. I spent a year or so asleep, or something like a deep sleep so that the faeries could heal me. I had lost my arm as well as my left eye. I can use and see out of my missing eye but sometimes, when the weather is humid in the human world, I ache with it. The same with my left leg. I didn't lose it, but it was close for a time. They made sure that I was whole and able to get around after I woke up." She told him how sorry she was. "I am as well. At the time, I had no idea why they had bothered to save me. I was, even back then, an immortal, and I wondered why they took the time and energy to make sure that I was whole. I'm glad they did now, with you being a part of my life now. But I would have been just as happy to have been left to die back then. I have actually thought that a great deal after I was healed. More so before I met you. Being an immortal didn't mean that I would die eventually if I wished it, but it did mean that I wouldn't be healed with my parts being reattached. I'm so glad for that now."

"You were with Adam's mate when she passed, I heard." They talked about the battles that he'd been in. Brad even removed his shirt to show

Becka some of the scars he had while doing battles for other realms. He told her that he and Adam's mate were the best of friends, even with her being a dragon and him only a human who was gifted with magic. He smiled then. "I'd like to see the other realms. Just to see their differences. Allison told me that there are a great many of them, but only this one is the one that you can access Earth by. So exciting to know that, don't you think?"

"Oh yes. Many differences. There is one realm, one that I don't visit all that often that is solely water. It's for the water creatures, of course, and once I leave there, I have to recuperate for several days before I can go back to the human world. It's been pointed out that I have to literally drown to be there. As you can imagine, it's a very scary place to be. Like here they have dragons, ones under the water that no one has ever seen before. The place protects them as much as they're protected here." She laughed, then stopped when a group of brownies flew by them, seemingly in a hurry.

When he joined her, he and Becka shared a good joke about all the other realms that he'd been to. Even going so far as to make up stories just for her entertainment. Christ, he loved this woman. It was then that it occurred to him that he'd never told her that. So he decided it was well past the time that he did.

"Becka, I love you dearly. I don't know that I have ever loved anything or anyone as much as I do you." She put her forehead onto his and told him that she loved him as well. "I'm so glad. I think that we have put off sleeping together long enough. How about you and I stay here tonight? I'll let Hamish and the others know where we are and have us some fun."

"If by fun, you mean sex, then I've been told several times today that I need to get laid. I am all for that." He asked her who had said that to her. "Allison. Several times, as a matter of fact. She told me it would make me less cranky."

Brad laughed. And he laughed more. He continued to laugh at her every time he looked at her pink cheeks and thought of her being embarrassed. The trouble was, he thought, was that Hamish and Lander had told him the same thing. Hamish was much nicer and more polite about it, but he loved them all the same. Lander was to the point about it, and he had felt himself being embarrassed as well.

Chapter 5

She'd never been wooed before. Never had a man that she barely knew touch her the way that Brad was now. His hands, warm from his magic, seemed to melt away her embarrassment and fears. Her body, especially around men that she didn't know well, just felt softer with his touch. As if he could sense her tensions and was able to smooth them away.

"Your skin is so soft. I love the way you smell, too. Like sunshine and the earth all in one." His words were like silk in the way that they touched her skin. His breath, hot and delicious smelling had her wanting everything from him. Even if she didn't know what that was just yet, she knew that Brad would be the only one who could give it to her. "I need to kiss you, Becka. Everywhere that I can."

Her clothing seemed to just melt away. If not for the cool breeze of his breath as he suckled at her nipple, she might have thought that it was all a dream that she was having, the best sexually fueled dream she'd ever had. Lying back on the bed when Brad asked her to, Becka wasn't embarrassed that he was staring at her naked. Not the fact that his cock, straining hard against his jeans, was making a stain at his zipper.

Brad touched her everywhere. With her newfound freedom with her body, she let herself make any noises that she did aloud. Telling him with her moans and sighs how much she was enjoying being made love to by him.

When he was at her pussy, her body suddenly tightened up. His small chuckle made her close her legs tighter around his head until he begged to be freed. When his hand lifted her up from the bed ever so slightly, her breath went out of her body in one woosh as his mouth covered her pussy, and he suckled.

She couldn't breathe one second and then felt as if her heart was going to shatter in the next.

His mouth was doing wonderful things to her, his tongue exploring a part of her that she'd never touched herself. Even as she rode his mouth and fingers, them sliding in and out of her with such speed that she cried out several times when she was close to coming, Becka let herself ride the waves of pleasure, still feeling like she was missing something. Something very important.

"You have such a wonderful taste about you, love. Come for me so that I can drink you down. Enjoy your flavor and essence like I want." His words were doing things to her that went beyond his hands. As he slid his fingers deeper and deeper into her, he would touch something, the one sweet spot she knew of that would set her off just enough to make her want more.

Even with the tiny climaxes she was having, jolts to her heart and mind that would have her crying out loud, Becka needed, no, she needed more than her next breath. Every time that he touched her, Becka would beg him for a release that he was keeping her from. Finally having enough, she pulled his hair up and jerked his head from her.

She thought it the most sexy thing she'd

ever seen with him leaning over her pussy, his chin and cheeks soaked with her juices. His eyes, glazed over, had her begging him for more than... whatever it was, she knew that they both needed it. Begging him to take her, he slowly released her legs and made his way up her length.

"Your thighs taste like the finest flowers. Your pussy?" He dove into her once more, she supposed in the event that she might have forgotten that he was eating her. "Your pussy is divine. I love how you soak my mouth with yourself. How your cream fills me and slides down the back of my throat. You make me want more."

"I need more, too. Oh, Brad, I love you so very much. I think I've been waiting for you forever. I do love you."

Brad continued to make his way up her body. Taking his time to touch places on her that he'd not touched before. A rib here. A small scar that she had on her hip from when a locking bolt slipped from her hand. He touched her breasts, lingering long and tirelessly while suckling at her nipples. Even her navel was given attention with his mouth and fingers.

"Please? Brad, please take me." Still, he

took his time. When he nibbled at her neck, her shoulders, she was sure that her pussy gushed more of her cream on the bed. Becka didn't care, didn't think beyond how close he was to filling her. Asking him one more time to take her, she could feel his cock at her entrance.

"I want to take you slowly and hard. I want to make you mine forever and fill you with a child. Tell me, Becka. Tell me again how much you love me." Even before she could draw in a breath to tell him anything, he entered her to his hilt. His balls, hot and full, were touching her while he paused just long enough for her to hear his heart pounding. His breaths, hot and short, were there for her to hear, too.

Becka felt her body adjusting to him. He was thick and hard, and her body was moving in a way that had him crying out. He now was doing the begging as she wanted to make him take her. But instead, she listened to what he was saying.

"You're so tight around me I can't move. Christ, what a way to die. I could, too. Just like this. My cock buried so deep inside of you that— oh Christ, Becka, I can't hold back anymore."

It was like he had become demented in

taking her. The bed banged loudly against the wall as he pounded her. Even as she reached up and wrapped her fingers around his shoulders, her legs lifted and wrapped around his hips. Crying out, uncaring if anyone heard her, she screamed loud and long when he told her he was coming. That was all it took, just him saying those two words that had her grabbing onto him tightly and thinking that she was never going to be the same again.

When she woke, not even sure how long she'd been out, Brad was still stroking her from the inside and out. His hands danced along her skin while his cock slowly fucked her. Each place his mouth touched her, his tongue would lick the spot where he had only just nipped at her flesh. Rising up, showing him what she wanted in the way of completion, Becka felt her body rise up off the bed at her hips and felt like she was pulling him tighter into her. Then she came.

Her body felt turned inside out. Then, she was taken through a hole in the air that took away all her breath, blood, and skin. As it was now, she wasn't sure that anything was going back on her body in the right places.

Becka was overly sensitive. Even his breath along her throat made her feel as if he was burning her alive, but strangely, in a good way. Crying out when she peaked, no other word for it, Becka was positive that she was never going to be the same no matter what kind of magic there was to put her back together again. She fell over a cliff of sensations that were hers and hers alone that she was thrilled to be sharing with the one true love of her life. Brad Kirk.

Waking up, the room was bright with light, which was the only reason that she knew that it was morning. Well, daytime, anyway. Brad was still in bed, too, but he was dressed in a pair of jeans that she'd never seen him wear before. Rolling over, he asked her if she was all right.

"I don't know. Ask me in a few minutes." He laughed and handed her a glass of some amber liquid when she sat up a little more. "I don't drink, but whatever this is sounds good."

"It's juice. The glass will refill itself for you. It's the least that I could do for you since you nearly killed me. Christ, I loved every part of that. But you've taken all of everything out of me." She nearly snorted a mouth full of the best-tasting apple juice she'd ever drank. "Laugh it up, but unless you're carrying my child right now, it might be a long time before we have any children."

She was laughing when he got out of bed after finishing off two glasses of the juice. When he held onto the bottom of the bed, it sent her into giggles. However, they were short-lived when she realized how sore she was, too. Getting up when he came out of the bathroom, she decided that she needed a shower. It wouldn't just clean her up but hopefully work out some of the soreness she was feeling.

By the time she was dressed, Becka wanted to return to the bed. Brad had left her, telling her that he had a meeting with Adam today that he couldn't miss. She, too, had places to be, but she had to make sure that Toby was all right. She'd not thought of him once last night before going to bed.

"I'm fine. I'm staying at the pack buildings so that I could get there when the test results come in." She told him she'd forgotten about that. "So did I, to be honest. If not for one of the professors reminding me, I would have been there in the other realm with you and Brad. Do you suppose he'd mind very much if I call him dad? It's just something that occurred to me. Anyway, the furniture arrived about an hour ago, and the pack helped them move it all into the house. We did a good job, considering it was nearly midnight when we finished up."

"I think that Brad would be beyond thrilled if you were to call him dad. I have a few things that I need to talk to you about, too." He asked her if she wanted to live in the other realm as much as he did. "Yes. I think that the three of us would enjoy that. But we'd have to maintain a residence there so that there isn't any trouble with you going to college and becoming a productive bear. Have you given much thought to what Calhoun asked you? It's a big decision for you to be making."

They wanted him to co-teach a couple of classes at the pack. He knew several languages, the same that she did and they wanted him to help with the pronunciation of it taught in the classes. Which she thought made sense. If you only learned from a book, how good did you think you were if you'd not heard anyone saying it aloud before. She'd learned that from someone she'd met while traveling.

"I told him what you said. That so long as

it didn't interfere with my school work, then I'd be happy to do it. I think that doing that will also make my language a good deal stronger than it is right now. What do you think?" She said that it was his decision, but she had thought the same thing. "Good. And I know we never discussed it, but I will tell you this. I'm so happy that you have Brad after I'm gone. I did really worry about you. But I feel like you have someone to hang around with and won't just do the driving thing for something to do. Like you said, you're getting much too old to be traipsing around the states like you are."

He was laughing when what he said to her occurred to her. The little shit was going to pay for that. And even with her threatening him, he still laughed harder at her. By the time they were both calmed down, he told her that he hurt a little from laughing so hard.

"I love you, Mom. So very much. And I know that my mom was your sister. I don't know that I would have turned out half as good as people say I would have without your help and influence." He laughed a little, but she could hear a bit of sadness in his voice as he continued. "You are what you learn, I've heard said about people. And I believe that I've learned from the very best with you in my life."

"Oh, Toby. I do love you." He told her how much longer he was going to be at the pack house and asked her if she and his dad, the first time she'd ever heard him say that, could meet him for dinner in town. Then he told her about this girl who worked at the diner and that he wanted to go out with her on his first date.

"I'm going to be glad that Brad is with me, aren't I? I'm going to be a sobbing mess when you take off with another woman and marrying yourself off." He told her that he was just hanging out with her, nothing more. "Right now, you say that. In a few years, you'll be getting laid and everything."

"Christ, I hope so. The every part sounds good, too." She was laughing again as they were hanging up. All she wanted to do was ask one of the women in the family to find out all they could about this other woman. She'd have to have Brad talk to him about women and money. There was a great deal of that stuff, marrying for some sort of payoff in the end, so she didn't want him to be suckered. She knew a lot of people that had happened to. Women or men marrying someone simply to divorce them later for a huge chunk of money. It sounded like she was jaded, but she was also old enough to know that it could happen to anyone.

~*~

"I don't think you're taking this job seriously. I'm offering you the job of a lifetime, and you're laughing at me." Becka assured Sarah that she wasn't laughing at her but laughing at the thought of her being in charge of so many little people. "Well, yes, I did point out that they'll be like children. But good children that wish to please and to do a good job for you. I didn't mention it to any of them, but I would imagine that you're going to have your hands full with them. Okay, now that I think about it, I can understand why you are laughing. It is funny. You will be in charge of thousands of children, like people who are thousands of years old. Goodness. I don't know that I'd take that job on."

They both laughed. Becka had been staying in the other realm with Brad for the last several days. It had been fixed up that Toby could come and go as he pleased, which made them both very happy. The fact that he was still traveling back and forth from the local college was keeping Toby happy as well. She'd never been so proud of anything as she was him at the moment. Thinking about him and how his parents would feel made her sad at how much they had missed.

As it turned out, Toby had been able to skip his freshman year of college altogether. Not only that, but he'd been able to test out of some English classes because of him knowing four other languages as well as a few math classes. He'd always been a great reader, too, so that had given him an advance on a few other classes that were going to be required of him.

Brad was acting like he'd really fathered Toby by walking around telling everyone that he met, some of them more than once, how his son was brilliant and, at only sixteen, was now a junior in college. Toby was more embarrassed than happy. He'd never been one to like a lot of attention paid to him.

"Are you going to take it?" After pretending that she had to think about it, she told Sarah that they both would. Brad was going to teach them some very outdated swordplay, having been a man who had carried one before in his lifetime, while she was going to keep them busy. It was a lot, she knew that, but right now, all she wanted to focus on was how happy she was with them living the way that they were. Traveling between the two realms was fun, too. And she was learning a great deal by being in both places.

Chapter 6

Calhoun wasn't happy about being roped into going with his good friend to meet with his client. He had to have a witness, and Calhoun had been the only one who had been free. He hadn't been, but with him working for himself, he was able to shift things around and be there for him. Brad had also asked him to evaluate the elderly woman, making sure that her changing her will wasn't going to be brought into question. That he'd done a great deal. It seemed to him that very few people were as trusting as they once might have been. Knocking on the door, he straightened up, adjusting his tie as he did so. The younger woman at the door asked them what they wanted. Brad did the talking while he made sure that they weren't going to be ambushed while waiting for the door to be opened wider for them.

"Hello. I'm here to talk to Ms. Brandon. I'm here to change her will around. We've spoken on the phone a great deal over the last few days." The door opened wider, and he could see the gun pointed downward toward the floor. The woman wasn't taking any changes, it seemed.

"You must be Margaret Jane." She said that it wasn't her but her sister. And to call her DJ, but her name was Diana June. "All right. Can we come in and get started on this? There is a great deal of paperwork to be done, and I know that Ms. Brandon is wanting to get this finished up before she goes into the hospital. I don't blame her for wanting things to be finished up. But that sort of surgery is done a great deal lately and I doubt that she'll have any issues. I'm to understand that she's having open heart surgery next week. Oh, my name is Brad Kirk. I spoke to her about having a psychiatrist to come to see her, too. That will eliminate the possibility that she isn't of sound mind when the will changes come into question. Like I told her on the phone, my name is Brad Curt. I've been an attorney for several years."

Calhoun had been told that his expertise as a doctor was needed. He'd also been briefed, very briefly, as it turned out, before coming here. While he didn't know what the family was like, he decided that he wasn't going to be making any kind of speculations until he had all the facts. Something that he liked having when he was dealing with people left out of wills. When they were invited in, the gun that the younger woman carried was put in the holster that was along her shoulder. It was Brad who asked her if she carried all the time.

"Usually not when I'm home. But I don't trust anyone enough, mostly my relatives like my father, uncle, and brothers, not to come barging in here where they're not invited. I will have no trouble blowing your brains out if you fuck around with my grannie. Understand?" They both said that they did. "All right, let's get this shit show on the road, shall we?"

It was Calhoun who asked the other woman how much the family had been in the house and what they did when they got inside. So far, DJ told him they'd not been able to breach the door, but that didn't mean that they wouldn't continue trying.

"So. Don't upset her, please. She's been having a rough time with it, and I would like her not to worry about what's going to happen to her." The woman's entire demeanor changed as soon as the gun was put away. Like she was an entirely different woman. "Grannie is in the living room, watching her soaps. As soon as it's over, she'll be able to talk to the two of you. Would you like a tea? Perhaps something to eat? Grannie made scones just yesterday, and they're delicious."

"I'd love a scone and a cup of tea if it's not too much trouble. Calhoun? Want anything?" He said he'd have the same. "What soap does your grannie watch? I got hooked on one while I was recuperating a few weeks back."

He just stared at Brad. He was acting strange himself. Reaching out to him, he asked him what the hell he was going on about. What he told him had him having to suppress his own bit of laughter, too.

"The grannie is also carrying a weapon. I was told, in no uncertain terms, that she will use it if provoked. I don't want to be shot if you don't mind. I've only just found my mate, and I'm having a good time getting laid

on a regular basis. Not to mention fun just hanging around with her and my son." Calhoun asked him what all the guns were for. *"They weren't kidding when they mentioned the brother and grandsons. The family is not the nicest people in the world, and she's put them in the hospital a couple of times when they decided that she wasn't going to die like they wanted. I kid you not, Calhoun, they were recorded saying that to her when she'd put one of them in the ER. Knocked his head into the wall, causing all kinds of wounds. DJ called me the other day and made certain that I wasn't going to bullshit her, either. I told you this. Remember?"*

"I do. Yes, but I thought...never mind. I'll behave." When they were shown to the living room, he nearly burst out laughing. Whatever he had expected, it wasn't the sight that he was seeing now.

There sat, in one of the biggest bright pink recliners he'd ever seen, the most un-grannie-like woman that he'd ever encountered. Laughing a little more, she turned to look at him and winked. It was all he could do not to go to her, pick her up, and hug the stuffing out of her. However, he felt like if he did that, he'd be in about as much trouble as he'd ever been with his own grannie. Smiling at her, he prudently waited for a commercial to come on before speaking to the elderly woman. However, she spoke first.

"You here to give me one of them there head tests? I'll tell you right now, I'm not a pushover. Nor am I like any of them old women down at the nursing home. Christ, oh Lord, they're nothing like I am, thankfully. I still like to get out and have me some fun even if I am ninety-three years old. If I ever get stuck in one of them, you might as well blow my head off. I won't last a durn day there. Mushy food. Mushy people and the most uncomfortable chairs I durn near ever sat my fat keister in. What are you anyway?" He told her that he was a psychiatrist. "No, I mean, what are you? Not human, that's for sure. I'm thinking…No. I was gonna say wolf, but you're not one of them, are you? Too tall. I knew me one of them wolf shifters once. Best lay I've had in my life. Durn, but he knew all the right spots to touch for me." Her cackling had him laughing, too. However, he wasn't sure if he believed her or not. Nor was he going to ask her.

"Bear. I'm a bear shifter. The very first of my kind. My mate and I are the king and queen of all bears, too, if that's something that you'd like to know." She nodded, then sort of tuned him out. With her show on, as she called it, he was free to look around the rooms he could see.

There were the remnants of a cake, chocolate if he didn't miss his bet on the dining room table that he could see from where he was seated. It, the table, and the cake had seen better days, but he'd bet that the cake had been homemade. And delicious, too. There were candles spread out on the table, too, and some plates with small bits of icing on them that he wouldn't have missed for the world if that had been his plate. It was his favorite part of all the treat.

When he heard Ms. Brandon clear her throat, he smiled and looked at her. Might as well get things going, he thought to himself. Again, she beat him to it. She was beginning to grow on him, and he decided that he really liked her. Even if they'd only exchanged a few words.

"I want to change my will around. I don't have all that much. A few acres of land that I rent out to farmers when I can. Don't charge them all that much. And they more than make up for it with all the fresh stuff they make sure I have. Gotta have fresh roughage, or as an old fogie, I might not be able to take a good poop when I need one." He laughed again. "Them boys of mine, they got no more sense than a rock if you ask me. Just the other day, one of them, Andrew, is his name. He told me that I've been hanging around long enough. That I should get to dying so he can have my money. Can you imagine saying that to your own mother? Not me. She would have knocked me three ways to Sunday. Anyway, I just stared him down with my gun pointed at the most useless part of him. His head. Don't even hold a bit of brain up there. Might well be his wiener is where the dummy keeps his brain, but I don't get into that with him no more. Stupid ingrate."

They enjoyed the next show together. DJ brought them a plate of scones that were so good that he ate two of them before he was able to have his tea cooled off enough to drink it. It was good, too. Calhoun had loved that they'd not put any sugar in his cup so that the scone wouldn't make it sweeter. Few people knew that about eating sweets with unsweetened tea.

He talked to both women, and they had a good time. When it was all said and done, Calhoun decided that she was about as sound of mine as anyone that he knew. More than likely more than most of the rest of her family. About the time her last show was over, Calhoun was calling her grannie, and she was calling him Cal. It was not a name that he particularly cared for growing up, but he didn't mind being called that by Mitsy.

He imagined that she might well have been around when things were flush with her family. While the house needed some repair work, it wasn't a dump. No dust in any of the corners, nor did he see any cobwebs, something that elderly people tended to forget about when they lived alone. There were dishes, too, neatly stacked in the China cabinet with matching glasses and other items. He, too, had a set of dishes, long packed away, that he'd have to find and give to Ruby. She might get a kick out of them. He knew that he would again.

After Brad joined them, his file that he'd brought handed over to her, the two of them talked about the changes that she wanted and how her estate, which, as she had pointed out to him, wasn't that much. After not getting all that far into the work, she asked them to wait for her granddaughter to show up so that she could be a witness to the paperwork. DJ was there, but she didn't want to be the witness as she lived with her grannie, taking care of her and keeping her safe. She didn't want anyone to say that she had been made to change things to suit her.

Yes, Calhoun could see that happening, too. Their family seemed to know all the angles in getting things to work in their favor. He was sure that there were other tricks that they used too that would get them whatever they wanted in the way of government handouts as well.

"They all think I'm about loopy. I'm not. Got a brain in my noodle that serves me well. MJ, my other granddaughter she's got the same curse that I do. Don't have to study up on things but to read it or hear it and it's there forever. Should have seen that little one going to school with her sister and ticking off them teachers. Most of them didn't have any more brains than my son does, but they were getting paid to get it wrong, and MJ wasn't having it. She's a good girl. Both of them are." DJ laughed, too, then, saying that she had inherited it as well, but not to the degree that her grannie and sister did. "Ah, but you're a smart cookie, aren't you, sweetie? I knew in my heart that the two of you would have trouble as soon as you were born. And I think that MJ is…well, she's handling it much better than I would. Her being smart and all."

"Do both girls live with you?" She said that it was only DJ, but MJ provided for her. "That's nice. For all of you, I'm betting." Brad joined them in the kitchen a few minutes later. The file that he'd brought with him was marked with colorful tags in places that he said he wanted to go over for her.

She said that was fine, but if he waited, he would only have to go over it the one time as MJ would be here. Brad said that he'd wait, but they'd have to do something for her while waiting. Neither of them was used to just sitting around on their duffs when there were pretty women to impress. Mitsy laughed with them.

"You boys. I swear to you. You know how to treat an old lady." They both claimed they didn't know anyone who was old, and that made her blush. "Go on with you now. DJ will have a little bit of work for you if you ask her. She's a good girl, that one, and has given up a lot to hang out with me all day. I would imagine that if MJ had been able to do this, she'd be here too, living with the two of us."

Mitsy was a very nice woman, and anyone who thought she was off her rocker had never taken the time to get to know her, he realized. She was smart and charming. A couple of qualities that few people had nowadays.

"We'll make up some dinner while we wait. The girls had a birthday just a few days ago. Twins, you see. I couldn't love them any more than if there were fifty of them. But MJ and DJ have been good for me — better than them durned sons of mine. But that's all right. They'll straighten up or else. Them girls will keep them in line." He didn't know if they could or not and decided that he'd have a few of his sloth hanging around close in the event that they might need it.

There were pork chops in the freezer that he was going to grill for them all. Brad was set to peeling taters, not potatoes, he was told, but taters. DJ came back from her outing, she had been out to get her nails done — Calhoun suspected that she'd been meeting a man. She smelled different than when she'd left, and she seemed less stressed. Of course, no one said a word to her about her nails either. They were neither painted nor smoothed out. Calhoun liked DJ too and would dare anyone to say a word differently about where she'd been the last couple of hours.

Around about six, they were all getting the table set up with plates and glasses when there was a rumbling sound that had him thinking he needed to run for cover. There was only one thing that sounded like that, and it made him wonder what the hell a helicopter was doing when flying so low around here. Just as he was going to ask if that happened often, he glanced out the kitchen window and watched the sucker land in the back field and two people get out while it was still running.

"That'll be MJ." Mitsy smiled and said that they'd told her they'd have her home by six. "They know better than to mess with her or me. I'm glad to see that they've kept their promise. It'll bring them boys a running, but that's okay, too. With all of you here, I'll be as safe as I can."

This is where I will start writing again. Anything beyond here won't be the same, I hope, anyway.

The person standing low and talking to

someone in the chopper still was dressed in fatigues. They were brown, dessert colors, and he could see that the other person was dressed more formally. Before the second person got back in the chopper, he turned and waved at them before getting back inside, and the first person began running toward the house, holding onto their hat that would have surely taken off in the force of wind from the blades still going fast enough not to be able to make out.

Calhoun watched the person making their way out of the blade's proximity while also keeping an eye out for anything else that might be in the way. Just the way that they were bent over made him think that they had been on a chopper numerous times, and simply didn't think about the fact that the thing could take a person's head off without any effort. When the person he could see it was a woman now, who was several feet from him, it was all he could do not to gap at her.

Dropping everything that he had in his hands, his body automatically stiffened up, and his right hand went to his forehead and a salute that he'd never forget. Watching as she stopped long enough to salute the chopper as it took off, she turned and did the same to him and Brad, who had saluted as well. Christ, oh mighty, he thought, she wasn't just army like he'd been lead to believe, but a god damned general.

"You're going to piss her off if you keep standing there." Mitsy laughed and stood up to meet her granddaughter. "Hello, darling. I have missed you. She won't say it, but DJ did, too."

"Grannie? Are these men treating you right?" She told the general that they were as good as gold. "If you say so. However, we have a lot to get done before my dad and uncles show up. Couldn't get here any other way than flying. Next time, I will try and get here quieter." Following them into the house, Brad stopped him before he could grab the door when it started to shut. He asked him what was wrong.

"General? She's a damned General? What the hell? Why weren't we told?" DJ laughed and said that they wouldn't have believed her if she had. No one ever believes that there is a woman general. "I guess that's about correct. But she is a very beautiful one and your identical twin, I'm thinking."

DJ was still laughing at Brad when she

went into the house after picking up her sister's luggage. He didn't even try and take it from her, there was no way that either of these women were going to be a pushover, and he wondered at that as well. Why did their uncles and father think that— well, Calhoun thought, this was going to be a fun thing to watch. He only hoped that they would show up while he was around. Might be the best entertainment he'd had in a very long time.

~*~

It didn't take long for the family to show up. Brad had to work especially hard to keep them all still alive by the time the police were called, but he was able to get the will filed, and the other paperwork finished up and put away, too. It didn't seem to him like there was much to the estate, but it was up for grabs as to who wanted it more. Any of the four sons would fight to the death for it, he'd seen but as for Grannie, she certainly wasn't going to let it go to any of them since she had such lovely granddaughters.

It had shocked him to see the women together. MJ and DJ were identical looking but that was all that they were alike about. While DJ could be hard, he noticed that it was MJ who seemed to command the power to make the other men do what she told them. Her pulling her gun on her father had made all of them laugh, but it had nearly turned deadly when the dad of the twins drew back to hit the elderly Brandon. Christ, he'd never seen anyone move so quickly as he'd seen the women move as one to stand in front of their beloved Grannie.

"You really want to rethink your next move, father. I won't have any trouble whatsoever burying you in a shallow grave out back. Dead or alive, it makes little difference to me. I've had plenty of practice at it, and I'm always armed with not just a bullet with your name on it but a handy shovel, too." Brad watched as MJ racked her glock and caught the bullet midflight as it shot out of the chamber. Then she set it on the table. And sure enough, it had her father's name on it in bold print. He could hardly tear his eyes away from the ammo so that he could see what the older man would do now. Her father called her an ungrateful, rude, useless woman. "Better that than a fucking bastard of a man who couldn't take care that his own wife and children didn't have to go without. I do wonder at times what it was that you did with the money that was mothers? Did you spend it on your whores, or did you drink it all away? If you tell me that you saved it for us, then I'll not believe you. You couldn't save your dick from getting hurt when you did have a job. How long ago was that now since you've been able to get that fucking thing up? I guess it's been at least twenty years now."

"You leave my dick out of this, Margaret Jane. And I'll have you not going around telling lies about me either. Keep your damned mouth shut before I shut it for you. In a permanent way, too." She laughed. It didn't sound like she had found anything at all to be happy about. Her voice nearly dripped with sarcasm. It actually made the hair on his arms and neck dance, she had conveyed it so well. "You hear me, girl? You'd best be listening to me before you get what your mother did."

"I'm not the least bit afraid of you." DJ stepped in front of her father with her back to her sister. She didn't say anything, but it did take him a full five minutes to realize that DJ had a gun pointed right at her father's gut. He'd not seen it, for the man had a large hang over his belt belly that he wondered how the man ever saw his dick anymore, much less use it.

When DJ told her father to go, he kept staring at MJ. The light in her eyes, the power of her anger, had him putting his hand on his own weapon. He knew that there was going to be bloodshed before the end of the evening. Brad did wonder how often they got into this sort of argument. No wonder they were all armed all the time. It was more than likely why the women in this family were still around. Not only were they all armed with guns, but he'd bet his last check that what MJ had told him about burying him in the backyard wasn't an idle threat either.

There wasn't much in the way of conversation on the way back to town. Brad knew that he was going to be peppered with questions about what had happened when he got home. Becka had wanted to go with him to the other home, but she'd been called away to help with a loaded truck that was stuck in traffic. It had been all over town that the Brandon women were hard on men. Also that they didn't have a sense of humor. That part he was able to say wasn't true. But not so much about them being hard on men. He'd been so stressed when he left that he'd slept all the way home.

"While I was in town, I heard from a couple of people that the low-flying chopper was MJ Brandon herself flying. Was that true?" He tried to think, and while he was doing that, Becka asked him if it was true that the two sisters looked a little alike. "They're supposed to be very intelligent as well."

"They look a great deal alike. Identical twins as a matter of fact." He thought about what Mitsy had said about them being so different that if they married their husbands wouldn't be able to tell them apart. He told Becka that. "I think that I could tell them apart if I had to. But it would be hard. Especially if they didn't speak. They're hard. Not just on men, like you said, but about themselves too. Also, and this is going to sound strange, but I think they're harder on themselves more than they are their father and four uncles. Who I've met, by the way."

"So have I. Just before the helicopter went overhead and to the field, the men were in the grocery store where I was picking up a couple of things. To be honest with you, I didn't even hear it go over it was so loud in the store. They were arguing with Mr. Kinkade about how much milk had gone up in the last fifteen years. Fifteen years. Like everything hasn't gone up over that period of time. Moron. Then they all four stiffened up and ran out of the place like it was on fire." He asked what she thought of it. "It said Army on the bottom of the helicopter so I just assumed that it was out on drills around here. I didn't know that it was going to land as soon as it was out of town."

"Did the Brandon men cause any trouble before they went to the house? I'm hoping that they'll behave themselves over the next week. Ms. Brandon has open heart surgery the day after tomorrow, and I'd hate for them to upset her before she goes in." Becka pulled a carrot out of the bag he'd just picked up from the store. Before she ate it, he pulled it out of her hand and peeled it for her then handed it back. "Thanks. I've never had a lot to do with them, the Brandon men, I mean. From what I've heard, they can be about as evil as the devil himself. What do you think?"

"I don't know. They're afraid of the girls, that's for sure. And when Mitzy pulled out her gun and aimed it at the ceiling, firing two rounds in the upper floors, they scrambled out of the house like they were on fire." The two of them laughed about that. He was glad to see that Becka was in a better mood than she'd been before. When Toby came in from work, he'd gotten himself a part-time job just a few days ago. Becka told him what had gone on. The boy looked like he'd shot up about a foot since he'd been living here.

Brad loved both Toby and his aunt Becka. Of course, Toby called his aunt his mom, and only a few people knew that he was her nephew rather than her son. But he didn't care so much as he loved him like he was his biological son and couldn't wait to hear someone call him dad. He'd talked it over with Becka a couple of times, but he'd not called him anything but Brad since they'd been married.

He'd been working in the yard for most of the afternoon. They had been living in the magical world for the last week and were having a good time scouting around for the things that Sarah had them looking for. For the most part, they've found very little trouble with the land or the house. Everything in their future it seemed hinged on Allison okaying them to live full-time in the realm the two of them did.

"I heard from Allison today." He sat back

down, thinking that he'd go back to work to keep his mind off of what was going on. "She has put her mark on us living here. She has a list of things that she wants us to do for the realm. Most of it was what Sarah had said we'd be doing. But keeping the faeries and the brownies busy all the time will certainly help keep them out of trouble. What do you think of being a babysitter for thousands and thousands of little people? I'm nervous about it, to be honest, but it's a job that I believe we'd be good at. Being able to have Toby come and go as we wish will make it easier on me."

"Me too. I couldn't do this and not see him when I can. He's a great kid, and I'd miss having a conversation with him. Not to mention watching the sports channels with him on the weekends." She agreed with him, and he pulled her into his arms. "Tell me what else she said. She really doesn't want us to do this, does she?"

"It's not that at all. No. She did give me a better understanding of the magic that we'd need to have. I've never thought of some of the other creatures wanting us to help them, too. But we're not to do that. She said that they have their own crews that can keep their people busy. It's hard enough for them to find something for the faeries to do in the middle of summer." She grinned up at him before continuing. "We're to have them start on getting the flowers and buds for the teas and drinks that they sponsor in the other world. I didn't know that the brew, as Sarah calls it, is an invention of one of the brownies."

He said that he thought that he'd had some once a while back. "It made me all hyped up so that I couldn't do anything but buzz around for a week after I drank it. I don't even remember the next two days after drinking it. But I have refused to have any since." Becka laughed, just as he'd hoped she would.

"Because you're not a faerie. This brownie, his name is Hoot, he liked to have a nice hot drink with his meal, and it had to be strong enough to make him sleepy at the end of his meal. Caffeine has the opposite effect on the faeries than it does on humans. Also, there are a few weeds that they'll collect for Allision, which she uses for a wrap when one of them is hurt. I guess it smells really bad. However, it doesn't do anything more than make them lie still while she puts it on their wounds. After they were lying still, she told me that she could have a good look at the wound and know just how to fix them up. It also works for small children who have a cough. The wrap has a horrid smell and taste, so having them lying down makes it so that they aren't required to eat it. Works all the time, she told me."

There were plenty of stories like that one. He'd heard a great many of them over the last several weeks while working around here. Mostly, it was falsehoods that were told to the faeries to have them rest. They would quite literally work themselves to death if they had a project given to them. That was a reason, too, that they needed a guiding hand, he and Becka, to keep them in line. He'd seen it happen on more than one occasion. The faeries were there to help and to please. Without someone telling them that they needn't work forever until it was finished, they would work round the clock to have someone happy about their project.

They had made a chart that would cover the four seasons. Actually, in this realm, there would be four seasons all the time. The beauty of the place made it so the faeries working with the fruit trees could give them a bit of downtime. The trees and the faeries. Also, and he thought this was a wonderful idea, there was also a time for vacations as well.

Each time that an area went dormant for the 'winter season,' it would be the time for the faeries and all the other creatures to have their downtime, too. It didn't happen, but twice a year for a week at a time per season. However, it was looked forward to and enjoyed by all, including the queens of the realm, who made sure that the weather was perfect for all to enjoy. They'd pack up their things, take a trip to one of the other seasons, and have a cookout or enjoy skiing—whatever their hearts desired, it was there for them to have fun with. Whatever sport or kind of vacation they wanted, they'd travel to that area and enjoy the freedom that they so craved.

That was another thing that they were going to be in charge of. Making sure that everyone took their allotted time off and rested up before going back to work.

There were doctors now who would care for any of the small creatures that were a part of the whole realm. It wasn't discussed much, but there was a great deal of depression that was rampant and more and more trouble between the areas. Sarah thought it was just boredom, but Becka said it was because there was too much competition between the groups, and that needed to be dealt with. Whatever it was, it was something that had to be taken care of soon, or it would get out of hand quickly.

They were just waiting on word to take over the job, and he knew that they'd work very hard for the queen and her sister. But not, as they were told, at the risk of their own health. He figured that they'd be watched over, too, by the two royal ladies of the realm.

Chapter 7

Marshall watched the meetings that were going on in the pack house. He didn't much care for the way that things were going, but he figured that he only had to come here once a month to pay his dues, and then that was it for another thirty days. When his name was called, he stood up and stretched. He hadn't realized that he had gotten stiff just sitting there.

"Are you trying to impress me?" He looked around to see who the man was talking to. "You, you fool. Making yourself look bigger because you had to wait your turn isn't going to get you anywhere with me."

"What's your beef? I've been sitting there—" He looked at the clock over the man's head and realized that it wasn't working. Figured. No one else was working either, so it was a perfect way to get out of work early. It was set at five when the hours of the pack house closed up. "I'm here to pay my dues. Then I'm going back to my home."

"You'll leave when I tell you to." Marshall didn't understand how Hamish and the others would talk about this place like it was a perfectly run machine. Every time he had to show up here, he was met with hostility and anger. "You're going to pay more for being a shit to me. I'm fining you a thousand dollars. To be paid in cash now before I'll allow you to leave."

Stretching his neck, hearing it pop a few times made him feel better. Right up until he was hit from behind. Turning on the person who dared to hit him, Marshall saw the gun before he did the man. It was then that he reached out to anyone that was nearby.

"I'm in a bit of trouble here. I can get myself out of it, but there is going to be — how on earth did you think that this place was a good pack? There has been nothing but arguments, backstabbing — about you, Hamish, and how this place would be better if all of you were dead. That wasn't told to me, but I've been in the

dickweeds head here". Hamish said that he was right outside the building and could come in right now. *"No. I mean, just stand out there and listen. As I said, I have a handle on what's going on in here. Just…just listen to how he talks about you."*

It was a shitty thing to do, but he really thought that the pack leader, Amish Shores, was playing everyone. When he handed over the dues, minus the fine that he wasn't going to pay, the man stood up. He understood at that moment that the man was a good deal shorter and rounder than he'd first thought.

"You listen here, you cheap piece of shit. I'm in charge here. And if you run to that pussy Hamish about what I'm saying and doing, who do you think he's going to believe? Me, that's who. I've been buttering up that moron for weeks now, and I'm going to own his ass as soon as I get that wife of his out of the way. Women shouldn't be able to go out and about like that one is." He laughed. "She just might find herself dead if she doesn't play well with me. Do you suppose she's a good lay? Don't answer that. She can't be. Christ, why are women acting like they're all that when men like me can cut them down in no time."

When the door behind him slammed against the wall next to it, Marshall didn't even turn to look. He knew who it was and wasn't the least bit surprised when Amish put his hand over his now missing throat. One thing you never did was talk about a mate to a vampire. Much less one that is the king of all their kind.

Hamish had ripped the man's throat out. Blood sprayed all over the room as his head, slipping down his chest, landed on the desk the man had been sitting behind. It looked like a trophy with his eyes wide open and an expression of disbelief written all over his face. Christ, this should have been done decades ago.

"Are you all right?" Nodding, he sat down when someone shoved a chair into his legs. He'd not realized how weak he was until then. Marshall didn't know if he could ever enter this building again without seeing all the blood. "Marshall? Look at me. Are you all right?"

"I don't know. Christ, I knew that he was a shit, but when he started going on about...did Launder hear this shit?" She kissed him on the cheek when she moved around to stand in front of him. "I'm so sorry, honey. I didn't know that he was going…how stupid do you have to be to say something like that to a good friend? Especially about his mate."

There was no reason for the police to be called. The man wasn't in good with them either. But within a few seconds, a pic of faeries showed up, and the area was cleaned of not just the blood but the body as well.

As they talked around him, Marshall got up and made his way outside. He was going to be sick and didn't want the others to know it. Tossing up his lunch and most of the bile on his stomach, he moved back to the pack house and sat on the steps. Breathing in and out, making sure that he wasn't smelling the blood or puke mess that he made, Marshall moved when the other two came out of the building. He just wanted to go home.

Waking up, finding himself in his big bed, he rolled to his side and tried to remember how he'd gotten here. Not that it mattered, he told himself. He was home and was feeling a good deal better than he had before. Dozing off and on, he decided to get up, shower, and start the rest of the day. It was nearing six in the evening when he entered the kitchen, where he noticed that most of the kiss gathered. Then he laughed. They asked him what was so funny.

"Vampire kiss meeting in the one place there is no need for them to have much less gather in. I never thought about how much we all gather in this one part of the house." A plate of food, mostly small things that he could eat with his fingers, was sat in front of him, and he was glad for it. Nothing breakfast-like. He didn't know if his belly could take that right now.

After eating, he made his way to the office that he'd been using when he needed to keep up on things for his business. Being an investment banker had made him and his friends a great deal of money over the years. And he was glad for it.

So many people who had been around for as long as he had were living off the streets. Having become bored with life in general, they stopped caring if they had money or even material things to depend on. He didn't want to be that person. The person who would stay with friends until he wore out his welcome, bouncing from home to home. Christ, his parents were like that. He wanted nothing to do with their lifestyle.

"I have a few things that I have to take care

of. I want you to know that I'll talk to the board for you if it comes to that. Not that I think it will. I hadn't any idea that...well, I can't thank you enough for helping me out with that. To think that I had allowed Toby to go over there and hang around. Not that I could have stopped the young man. He's a great deal like his mother in that respect." They both laughed. "I'll make arrangements to have the pack taken care of. I don't suppose you'd want to run it, would you?"

"No. And hell no. I have enough going on in my life that I don't need for you to add to it. Thanks for thinking of me, but nope. I don't want anything to do with that." Hamish said that he figured that was going to happen. Changing the subject, Marshall asked if there was anything that he could do to help around the town.

"Not yet, but come fall and into the winter, we'll need to be getting things for the people in town. Wood for fireplaces is a priority." He made a mental list for himself. Marshall did tell Hamish about the fallen trees that were clogging up the pack land, which he was sure someone would love to have gotten rid of. "I'll ask about that. Thanks. Are you all right?"

"I am. Thank you. And just so you're aware, I found myself a house. It's not on the market yet, but I'm hoping for it." He told him the address, and Hamish, of course, knew the home. "I'll probably be turned down for a loan. It wouldn't be the first time. But I can pay cash. Thanks very much for bringing me here, Hamish. I don't know what I would be doing if you'd not called."

"My pleasure. Now, if we can get you a mate, things will be much better. For all of us." Marshal didn't comment. He didn't much care for having a mate. He'd been married once, a long time ago, and hated to admit it, but he didn't want to ever go through that again.

Going to his room, Marshall decided that he was going to go to bed early. It had been a long couple of days, and he'd had enough stress. Lying on the bed, his body relaxing as he shut out the noise of the house, Marshall decided that he should do more of this. Taking to going to bed early and eating better. It certainly made his disposition a good deal better.

Before You Go...

HELP AN AUTHOR

write a review

THANK YOU!

Share your voice and help guide other readers to these wonderful books. Even if it's only a line or two, your reviews help readers discover the author's books so they can continue creating stories that you'll love. Log in to your favorite retailer and leave a review. Thank you.

AWARD WINNING, BESTSELLING AUTHOR

Kathi Barton, a winner of the Pinnacle Book Achievement Award and a best-selling author on Amazon and All Romance books, lives in Nashport, Ohio, with her husband, Paul. When not creating new worlds and romance, Kathi and her husband enjoy camping and going to auctions. She can also be seen at county fairs with her husband, an artist and potter.

Her muse, a cross between Jimmy Stewart and Hugh Jackman, brings her stories to life for her readers in a way that has them coming back time and again for more. Her favorite genre is paranormal romance, with a great deal of spice. You can visit Kathi online and drop her an email if you'd like. She loves hearing from her fans. aaronskiss@gmail.com.

Follow Kathi on her blog: http://kathisbartonauthor.blogspot.com/

www.ingramcontent.com/pod-product-compliance
Lightning Source LLC
Chambersburg PA
CBHW032006170626
46807CB00006B/2680